The Third Prince and the Enemy's Daughter

A Calliope Novel

By Alex McGilvery

The Third Prince and the Enemy's Daughter
By Alex McGilvery

Cover Design by A.P. Fuchs

ISBN 978-1-989092-27-9

Chapter 1 Return from the Hunt.

Roger stomped away from his father's Staal. The king had kicked him out before his brothers lost their tempers and beat him bloody. Roger didn't know what was more infuriating, his father's dismissal, or him protecting his youngest son. His brothers made no secret of their belief that his education in Anglia had made him soft.

"You've been home for two years." Chiza leaned against the wall of Roger's suite. "Haven't got very far."

"Not you too," Roger waved a hand. "Change is coming whether we want or not. The Empire is not going to ignore the wealth of our countries."

"There is change, then there is change." Chiza shrugged. "If your hunt is unsuccessful, you need to change your tactics."

"Maybe I should go back to Anglia." Roger paced through the room. "There isn't a place for me here."

"You may have forgotten, but there wasn't much of a place for you in Anglia."

"Maybe I should take a place on a steamship like Bundo." Roger grinned and pointed at Chiza. "I could run the engine and you could shovel coal."

"I expect you would find that captain harder on you than your father."

"You saw the way Cal charmed everyone in the market."

"Including you." Chiza crossed his arms. "Running away will not bring a good end to your hunt."

Roger paced through the room. His degree hung on the wall, oddities from Anglia occupied spaces on shelves and tables. His books gathered dust. The words didn't have the same power here at home.

He stared out the window, then closed his eyes. Maybe he should have left with her, assuming she would have let him. He'd worn that yellow suit, but she hadn't rolled her eyes or sneered at him like the people here, or in Anglia. They'd talked like equals. She'd been sympathetic, what was the thing she'd said to him? Something about his people needing him, not his education.

"Chiza, we're going hunting." Roger threw his suit off and dug his hunting clothes out of the trunk.

"Hunting?" Chiza raised an eyebrow.

"I need to do some thinking, and I can't do it here." Roger picked up his spear from where it leaned, neglected in a corner.

They left the staal, the guard didn't recognize Roger until she saw Chiza. Roger's legs ached by the time they made it to the jungle surrounding the city. He was out of shape. Once under the shade of the trees, he pushed everything out of his mind but the need to be aware of the animals around him.

They walked until the light faded, then ate what Chiza had brought. Roger had been in too much of a rush to think of food. *Am I truly a fool?*

Chiza nudged Roger away with a foot and they continued through the paths. Roger's feet remembered how to walk, and his ears began to pick up the sounds of life around him. *I should have done this sooner.* The only reason Roger could come up with why he didn't was he hadn't hunted in Anglia, at least not like this. His side ached and he rubbed an old scar.

The trail of a deer crossed their path and he followed it. The smell of water tickled his nostrils, so Roger curved around to come to the water from a different direction. When they'd arrived at the pool, Roger placed himself where he could see the trail down to the water and waited.

The daylight dimmed as they stood still as the trees. A deer hesitantly crept toward the water. Once it lowered its head to drink, Roger threw his spear and brought the animal down without it being able to do more than twitch.

"You haven't forgotten everything." Chiza punched his shoulder before striding over to the deer. He tossed Roger's spear back to him, then pulled out a knife to clean their kill.

The slight creak of a branch was the only warning Roger had of the leopard's attack. As the big cat leaped toward Chiza's back, Roger charged forward his spear pierced the cat's heart, pinning it to the ground. Chiza stood and checked the leopard.

"Clean strike." He frowned and started cleaning the second kill. "We should have known it was there."

"The hunt takes us in unexpected directions." Roger dabbed at the scratches on his chest. "We're Congu."

***

They walked into the staal, Chiza carrying the deer, Roger the leopard. The guard saluted them as they passed. The old huntmaster waved his approval when they left their catch with him.

"The king wished to see you when you returned."

Roger nodded and headed for his rooms. After donning the tunic and skirt of a Congu warrior, Roger allowed Chiza to lead him toward the King's Staal. As before, his father lounged on his seat, posture not hiding the deadliness of his gaze or abilities. Scars covered his gleaming dark body to attest to the battles he'd survived. Part of Roger's problem in this room was his lack of battle and hunting scars. His brothers stood like statues on either side of their father.

They each carried almost as many scars as his father. Neither of them so much as glanced at him. But his father smiled briefly. The scratches on Roger's chest itched.

"I see you begin to return to your people. It is good to see. Bring a stool and sit. I would speak with you."

"Yes, my king." Chiza handed him a folding stool which Roger set at the foot of the stairs up to the dais. He sat and bowed his head.

"What shall you do now that you have returned to the Congu?" The King's voice rumbled through the room, but the angry edge of their last conversation had vanished.

"My name is Roger Hrona Xanichi." Roger took a deep breath. *Your country needs who you are.* Cal's words rang in his head. "I have returned from my hunt; will you hear my tale?"

The Second Prince snickered, but it was cut off by a casual slap from the King which sent him staggering. He dropped to his knee.

"Forgive me, my King."

King Xanichi nodded very slightly and the Second Prince returned to his place.

"Speak."

"As you wish," Roger let out a careful sigh. "You sent me far across land and sea to learn of people who may prove enemies as quickly as friends. I lived among them and hunted their intentions. As with your Staal, there is disagreement. They have a law against conquering foreign lands, though many would have no problem setting it aside. You have heard stories of their strength and prowess, seen their ships sail our waters. Few of them are warriors as we would count warriors, but it would be a mistake to think them weak. We hunt the lion strength to strength, but how do we deal with a nest of volcano ants?"

"You think they are but ants?" The First Prince tilted his head.

"Yes and no, my brother." Roger chose his words carefully. "Like ants they are individually weak, I met no warrior who might challenge me, and you know I am not the strongest of my family." He smiled slightly. "Yet with their inventions and engines, they could be dangerous. An enemy who doesn't understand the hunt will be hard to face as we will know nothing of their intentions."

"All this I know," the King rumbled and shifted slightly. Roger was going to lose him. He had to risk everything on one throw of the bones.

"You wisely sent a scout to learn of them." Roger lifted his head and met his father's eyes. "Will you not hear my words and discern their value?" He dropped his head. "I admit I returned filled with pride not suiting my station. Forgive me and use me."

"Very well, my son. What is the single thing which threatens us the most?"

"Be patient, father, my answer may be a roundabout trail."

The King nodded.

"The Anglians trade with nations across the world. Even the people across the ocean who drove the Anglian ancestors from their shores. Their goods are like the cotus flower. A taste is only a taste, but the more one eats, the more one wants until it consumes all desires. You saw how hard it was for me to turn away."

The First Prince nodded at Roger. Encouragement from his eldest brother was a rare thing.

"Yet they sell their goods here and in other places. Some deal deliberately in ensnarement, but many are all unknowing. They don't know the taste of their own bloom."

"Like the red monkeys who guard cotus flowers." His middle brother spoke thoughtfully. None of Roger's family were fools, except perhaps him.

"Yes, but imagine if red monkeys were to trade for their flowers?" Roger stumbled over his words. *Slow down, you don't need to rush this hunt.*"

"Are you saying we shouldn't trade with them?" The King's hand brushed against a steel knife which had been a gift from an Anglian trader who'd asked to set up shop in their land.

"I think the time for closing our borders has long passed. But it doesn't mean we shouldn't think of brewing our antidote to their drug."

"Antidote?" The King raised his eyebrow slightly.

"There is nothing they sell us which we can't build ourselves. Don't mistake, they may seem like wizards with their engines and machines, but anyone can build them if they have the knowledge."

"Where would we get such knowledge?" The King sat up and leaned toward Roger. "I came close to losing my son to their wiles, shall I send more warriors to be entangled?"

"My King," Roger kept his hands still on his knees, though he wanted desperately to wipe his palms dry. "I believe we already have much of this knowledge. Many of our people have sailed with the Anglians or their allies, or their enemies the Kershian Empire. Those people may not know it themselves, but they are our answer. The answer to Anglian machines is not to pretend they don't exist, but to have Congu machines to match them."

In the silence which followed, Roger thought he'd pushed too far, too fast. Then the King laughed and jumped up from his seat. Roger stood quickly enough to send his stool skittering across the floor.

"Our ancestors had seats of learning. Warriors from across the world came to learn. Knowledge was as valued as spear." The King paced through the room waving his hands. "It is time once again."

"Father..." Roger choked on his words.

"What need do we have for machines?" The Second Prince spoke from the top of the dais.

"Imagine we do not build these engines, but the Sombi do." The First Prince spoke quietly. "Or worse they get addicted to the toys of the Locosians and these peddlers gain a foothold on the border of our land?"

"Worse than the engines are their guns." Roger said. "I know you have seen them. Rich Anglians brag of visiting Congu and hunting, though they troop through the jungle like so many baboons. They kill lions and elephants from great distances."

"They are cowards." The Second Prince snarled the words.

"They value the hunt differently from us." Roger winced at the glare his brother sent him.

"Roger is right." The King turned to face all three of his sons. "If these guns can kill a lion, they can kill a warrior. Yes, they may be cowards, but that only makes them more dangerous. If the Sombi arm their warriors with guns how long would we last?"

"Even the Sombi…" The First Prince trailed off. "They do a lot of trading with the Kershians. Word is they are building a railway into the interior of their land to make it easier for these pale folk to ravage the jungle and hills."

"Roger, find these people you speak of. Introduce them to Bhansin. Your brother will oversee the work, he will ask for your aid as he needs it. Whatever we can learn, but I want an answer to the Locosian's guns. I will not send warriors to die needlessly."

"And I?" The Second Prince frowned.

"You love our traditions; you have a passion for our people. You will work to be sure we don't lose ourselves in the dreams of the cotus flower."

***

Roger walked through the market with Chiza behind him. He'd said there would be Congu who had served on Anglian ships. He recalled Bundo, kneeling on the deck of the Kestrel. If only…

"There." Chiza brushed Roger's shoulder with his fingers. A man sat under a canopy. He wore clothes more like Roger's Anglian suits than traditional Congu garb. Roger wandered over to look at the man's wares.

They were an odd mix of knives of all sizes, then toothy circles of steel and other bits and pieces.

"How may I serve my Prince?" The man pushed himself to his feet, no, foot. His right leg ended just below his knee.

"Please sit." Roger sat smoothly on the stone while Chiza frowned at those who crowded close out of curiosity.

"I'm Bh'ob," the man said, "Of the Hcazo tribe."

"Well met Bh'ob." Roger smiled trying to set the man at ease. "My mother was Hcazo."

The man handed Roger a knife.

"I've been trying to make my own blades as fine as the ones the Anglians bring. Had some shore leave and spent it touring their factories. A shipmate had a brother who worked in one."

Roger tested the edge with his thumb. It didn't have the gleam of his father's blade, but had a rough beauty of its own.

"Chiza, what do you think?"

His bodyguard took the knife and examined it closely, using it to cut his forearm slightly. He nodded and passed the blade back to Roger.

"Chiza is impressed." Roger hefted the knife. "What did you use for the handle?"

"It is bone, my Prince." He picked up another knife. "A friend keeps them for me from the cattle he sells." The knife glinted slightly in his hand. "This one's shavo root." He passed it over. Roger examined it closely.

"What else besides knives do you build? He reluctantly put the knives back on the blanket.

"These are engine parts I'm playing with." Bh'ob put two together and showed how they fit.

"Could you build a whole engine?" Roger's heart skipped a beat.

"Not sure if I could," Bh'ob put the gears down. "But there's a fellow down in the lower town who built one. He uses it to cut lumber."

"Would you introduce me?" Roger leaned forward eagerly. "But not before you let me buy four of your knives. If you were to present one to the King, which would you choose?"

"This one." Bh'ob unwrapped a long thin shape. "It isn't pretty, the blade is more spear than knife. It was my first, but the handle is made from a lion's shoulder blade, from my first hunt."

Roger put his hand up and Chiza dropped a tiny bag into it.

"I will buy it and three others." Roger picked up the bone handled knife, the shavo root, and another bone one.

"I cannot sell this knife." Bh'ob bowed to the ground. "It is unworthy, but it holds a piece of my soul. I will give it to you to give to my King."

"I have a better idea." Roger stood and offered his hand to his fellow tribesman. "Gather your wares and you can present it yourself." He thought for a moment the other man was going to faint, but he nodded sharply and deftly packed everything away, then picked up two sticks and stood.

"My life is my King's to do with as he will."

Chiza took the bundle from Bh'ob. The man started to protest.

"You would not survive to carry a knife into the presence of the King, Chiza will guard your work with his life."

At the entrance to the Staal, Roger sent a message to his eldest brother that he wanted an audience with his father.

Bhansin came with the wrinkles on his forehead which warned the world he was not in a good mood.

"What do you want?" He glared at Roger, ignoring Chiza and Bh'ob.

"That knife that father likes, the one the trader gave him. Do you think he'd like to see one made by Congu hands?" Roger put his hand out and Chiza dropped one of the bone handled knives into his brother's hand.

Bhansin took even more time to peer at the knife and assess it. He reluctantly passed it back to Roger.

"Keep it, a gift from one brother to another." Roger grinned as he caught the flash of delight on his Bhansin's face.

"What's up?" Tcoza stomped up to them, not even trying to hide his scowl.

"I am bringing a gift for father." Roger put his hand out for the knife Chiza handed him. He gave an internal sigh, the other bone handled knife. Chiza could always read him like a book. "But first let me make a gift to my brother."

The Second prince took the knife and tested it while Roger watched grinning. "A trader knife, not as pretty as father's."

"A Congu blade made by my fellow tribesman, Bh'ob."

Tcoza peered at it again.

"You made this?" He waved it in Bh'ob's face.

"Yes, my Prince."

"Did you appease its soul?" Tcoza held the blade delicately.

"The old man who helped me get started taught me." Bh'ob held out his arm, covered in tiny scars.

"A blend of Congu and foreign." Tcoza nodded slowly at Roger. "You might be right about this after all. I accept your gift." He bowed slightly to Roger, then spun to walk away.

"Let's go see father before he comes to see for himself what all the fuss is about." Bhansin led the way into the room where the King sat on his seat tapping his fingers on the arm. Bh'ob bowed deeply.

"My King."

"Stand, my sons wouldn't have brought you here if you didn't have something important to tell me."

Bh'ob looked at Roger.

"It is death for one such as me to carry a blade in the presence of the King."

"Chiza will be your hands," Roger said, "I'm not about to lose you."

Chiza put the bundle on the floor and took out the wrapped knife. He carried it to the King while Roger dragged Bh'ob with him to the foot of the dais.

"We spoke of a Congu response to the traders' wares." Roger grinned broadly, though he tried to keep his face straight. Chiza put the cloth wrapped knife on the stone in front of the King and bowed himself back behind the princes.

The King picked it up and unwrapped the long thin blade. He ran his fingers across the handle and along the blade.

"It speaks to me of the hunt. This knife has a spirit my other one lacks." His eyes caught the blademaker like a lion holding a gazelle. "I accept your gift. You may say the King carries a blade you have fashioned." He pulled the trader knife from his belt and put it on the floor, then replaced it with the Congu blade.

"I'm sure you have already given your brothers gifts of these knives?" The King looked at Roger and for a second, he was trapped in the knowing gaze of his father.

"Yes," Roger stammered.

"Good. They will wear them with pride."

The King waved his hand in dismissal and Chiza led them out of the room.

Bh'ob leaned against a wall.

"I didn't fear so much facing a lion."

"You did well, Bh'ob." Bhansin slapped the man on his shoulder. "Now I want to know; can you teach others to work steel as you do?"

"Yes, yes, my Prince. It isn't far from what our smiths do now, only a few things I do different to make the steel harder and stronger."

"Good," Bhansin turned away. "You will start tomorrow. Roger, show him which gate to enter through and make sure the guards know him."

"Yes, brother." Roger clamped down on his glee to keep from dancing in the hall.

"Now, I'll show you around, then you take me to introduce the man with the engine."

Chapter Two A Mother's Plea

In the end, Roger and Chiza followed a young man down the hill. Voz'ci, Bh'ob's son.

"Father finds it hard to get up and down the hill."

"I can see that with his leg." Roger said.

Voz'ci laughed.

"No, he's learned to get around well enough on the one leg. Been a few years since he come off the ship, missing a leg and full to the brim with stories. His lungs aren't as good as they were. I think he should wear a mask in his shop, but he says it's too late for him, but he makes me wear one."

"I see." Roger glanced at Chiza who nodded slightly. Masks would be part of the shop in the Staal. They didn't want to lose Bh'ob too soon.

"This is a rough section of town." Voz'ci stopped a moment. "Stay close to me and you'll be fine."

"Very well." Roger's lips twitched. Bh'ob must have neglected to tell his son who he was guiding. Just as well, the young man was a fountain of information, pointing out disreputable dives and places one could buy the best fresh fish.

Roger heard the engine long before they came close to seeing it. Its regular thumping echoed through the streets. None of the other people paid any attention to the noise, so it had to have been running quite a while.

"Hoy, llathia, your father's got visitors." Voz'ci yelled at the gate into a yard surrounded by a high fence. The gate swung open and they walked through.

Llathia was a young woman, not much older than Voz'ci. She frowned at the intruders. Roger shook himself loose of the shock which had frozen him and smiled at llathia. She looked Sombi, her face reason enough for the fence.

"I'll take them back." She spoke Congu without an accent. Roger sensed Chiza on alert behind him, though he couldn't imagine any danger in this place.

She glided through stacks of wood and Roger could understand the fascination with which Voz'ci watched her.

"Papa, get out here, you've got visitors." She shouted loud enough to make Roger wince. "He's a little hard of hearing." She handed something to Roger. "You'll want to plug your ears when he shows off his engine."

Roger passed a pair of the wax balls to Chiza, Voz'ci abandoned them to follow Ilathia.

"Heh, well get yourself in here." A wizened old man stuck his head out the door reminding Roger of stories his mother used to tell him of forest dwellers not much bigger than monkeys. He walked through the door and immediately was grateful for the wax. As loud as the thing was outside it was a dozen times worse here.

"Come see the old girl." The old man skipped ahead and pointed to something so strange Roger had to shake his head and look again to see if his eyes weren't lying to him. The engine was made of wood. The boiler was a huge section of tree trunk with rope bound tightly around it. The pistons looked like trees hissing steam as a they drove another tree, trimmed down to be a shaft. Bands of cloth ran from the shaft to run machines, some were saws, but others did things Roger didn't immediately understand.

He compared this beast to the gleaming steel and brass engine on the Kestrel. He couldn't help laughing.

The old man didn't notice. He adjusted some things which made no difference Roger could see, then dragged them through the place to show them how the logs were sawn into lengths. Other saws cut them into long flat boards, then into narrower pieces. A machine smoothed out some boards so he could run his fingers along them with no fear of splinters. After the tour, the man pushed Roger and Chiza out the door and closed it behind him.

Roger looked at Chiza and started laughing again, until tears leaked from his eyes.

"He may be a crazy old man, but he's my father, and prince or not, you won't mock him." Llathia stood hands on her hips, glaring at Roger.

"Prince?" Voz'ci's voice squeaked.

"Pay attention." She smacked the back of his head. "to more than my backside."

"Hey, how did you know…"

llathia smacked him again, but she had a faint smile on her face.

"llathia." Roger bowed to her. "I apologize if you thought I mocked your father. I couldn't help but laugh I was so delighted. He is without a doubt a genius. Is there a place a little quieter we could talk?"

The young woman looked slightly mollified and led them back through the yard to a house Roger had missed seeing, the first time through. He admired its construction. Made entirely of boards from the sawmill.

Llathia opened the door and waited for them to pass before closing the door behind her. The sound of the engine reduced to a muffled thumping and Roger pulled the wax plugs from his ears.

"What does the Third Prince want with my father?" llathia banged around in the kitchen. "Mother, guests, put on your nice dress."

An old woman appeared from behind a curtain wearing a swath of beautifully dyed cloth. Where he'd looked like a forest goblin, she had the bearing of a queen.

"Welcome, Third Prince. I am nnontui."

She had some Sombi features and some Congu.

"I see you are puzzled. The royal family doesn't get up our way often. Mtuaka is our tribal chief, but we don't see much of him either. The truth is the Congu and Sombi have been raiding back and forth across the river for so long there isn't one of us who doesn't have the blood of both nations running through us."

"I see." Roger glanced at Ilathia who glowered at him. "As my father's son I should be above assumptions based on appearance." He bowed to Ilathia. *At least I'm getting good at apologizing.* "Forgive my rudeness."

"I understand." She slumped into a chair. "As I got older, father built that fence more to protect me, than his engine. The only Sombi woman on the streets are assumed to be for sale. I haven't been beyond the fence since I became a woman."

"I wasn't aware there were any Sombi in Lusundi."

"You wouldn't, would you, Third Prince?" The young woman's voice still carried an edge as sharp as the knife in Roger's belt. "So why did you come down this hill to visit my father?"

"The King has set me and my brothers to gathering Congu who can build machines for us, so we don't need to be entranced by the trader's goods." He placed his knife on the table. "Made by Voz'ci's father, the King was impressed."

"They are good. I have one in the kitchen."

Nnontui chuckled and shook her head.

"More listening, daughter, and less talk."

Llathia blushed dark and knelt in front of Roger.

"Forgive me, my Prince."

"You are forgiven, it is refreshing to have someone talk to me without quaking at the knees."

She stood and went back to the kitchen, returning with a tray set with cups and a plate of bread slices.

"It isn't much," llathia said, "but help yourself."

"nnontui makes the best bread in the city." Voz'ci reached for a slice, only to have his hand slapped.

Roger smiled and helped himself, then slid the plate toward the young man.

"It is excellent bread." He said after taking a bite. A few more bites and his slice was gone. He looked at the plate, maybe one more? After he and Voz'ci had demolished the bread and sipped the cool fruit juice in the cups, Roger sighed.

"I'm hoping your father could teach other Congu how to build his machine."

Llathia shook her head. "Not going to happen. If you'd asked even last year, he might have, but now, his whole world is that engine. Some days he doesn't recognize me." She ran a finger along a scar on her arm, then lifted her head and looked at Roger in challenge. "I could. Teach people about the machine. I've helped him work on every part of the thing. If he'd let me, I could make it run smoother."

"Would you then, come up the hill and teach?"

"Who would want to learn from me? I might as well be their enemy." Llathia straightened, but her hands shook.

"Chiza." Roger stood and waved his bodyguard forward.

"llathia, I can't guarantee no one will harass you, but I can promise no one will do it twice. I pledge my right arm to your service. Chiza will be your shadow until everyone sees the warrior in you and not the Sombi."

Llathia gasped and pulled back and looked up at Chiza. He nodded slightly and moved to stand behind her.

"Before you steal my daughter away." nnontui pointed at the Prince, "you must promise to do all you can to stop the raiding on the border. Mtuaka has no interest other than in taking his share of the plunder. The poor Sombi girls here belong to him. Worse, the last few months the young men have started using guns on their raids. Boys who once came home with scars now are buried in graves in the jungle with no marker to guide them home."

You will fulfill the request of the first person to ask you for help, no matter their station or the nature of the request.

Cal's 'punishment' of Chiza, one Roger had taken on himself thinking it would be a bit of fun. A chill ran down his spine. He could not refuse.

"I will do what is in my power, nnontui." Roger drew the knife Bh'ob had made, and ran its point across his arm, then put a dab of red on his forehead. "I swear on my life."

Nnontui and llathia dropped to their knees. Llathia open her mouth, then shut it. The oath had been spoken, and there was no taking it back.

Roger and Voz'ci walked up the hill. The young man as silent as he had been talkative on the way down. As they got to the wall of the Staal, he turned to face Roger.

"My prince, you have given your right arm to protect llathia, she is very precious to me. I'm not much, but I offer myself in his place until he returns to your side."

"Do you know what you are offering?" Roger held the young man's chin.

"I grew up in the city." Voz'ci met Roger's gaze. "But I have hunted."

"What?"

"A river horse." Voz'ci looked down as if he expected disdain.

"An honourable hunt." Roger said. "Come on then. First thing you must learn is only speak when we are alone."

Voz'ci nodded then followed Roger into the Staal.

Roger never paid attention to Chiza, the big man was always there and had an uncanny way of knowing what Roger was thinking. Having Voz'ci walking in Chiza's place unsettled him. No matter, it was done now.

Chapter 3 Blood Oath

A warrior knocked on the wall outside Roger's room. He put his head through the curtain.

"King would like to see you."

Roger jumped up and nodded to the woman, then nudged Voz'ci with a toe.

"Come on, we need to go see the King." He dressed while the young man dragged himself awake. By the time they stepped out into the hall, Voz'ci was alert enough to set himself at the proper distance from Roger. They'd spent much of the afternoon working on it. The young man had enthusiasm to spare, but his attention span wavered.

They stalked through deserted halls. Moonlight shining through windows created shadows. Roger noted that Voz'ci paid careful attention to the shadows, even in the King's Staal. He might work out better than Roger had hoped.

Two warriors stood outside the King's room, one pulled back the curtain, the other gave Roger a look of what might have been amusement, or pity.

The King sat straight on his chair, not a good sign. Two battle-scarred warriors stood where Roger's brothers normally were.

"I heard that you came in the gates with the mark of a blood oath on your forehead. When did you plan on informing your King of your actions?"

Roger prostrated himself in front of his father. To his relief, Voz'ci stood still and silent behind him. He didn't want the young man paying for Roger's foolishness.

"I am a fool, as you know, my King." Roger spoke into the stone floor. "I gave the oath in return for a person agreeing to come to teach our crafters how to build a steam engine." He would have pushed himself lower if the floor would have allowed.

"And Chiza?"

"The person is from Mtuaka's tribe, on the border with Sombi. She feared for her safety if she came unprotected."

"I see."

Roger lay still, waiting for the dire punishment to fall. His limbs began to shake.

"Oh, get up, son." His father's voice shifted from the hard words of a King, to the father who had personally taught Roger to use spear and shield in preparation for his first hunt. "You, the one standing in Chiza's place. Bring a stool for your prince, then one of the warriors in the hall will teach you to brew oath tea."

Roger almost fell to the floor again. He had yet to taste the oath tea. It would bind him to the King's word. If he betrayed the oath, not even being his father's son would save his life.

Voz'ci put a stool behind Roger, then padded out of the room.

"While we wait, tell me of this oath."

"I must start with meeting a ship's captain." Roger recalled the light-hearted way he'd taken the punishment on himself, not for an instant thinking of possible consequence. He winced at his stupidity. To his shock, his father reacted with laughter, not rage.

"This woman must have made a deep impression on you, to steal your ability to think so thoroughly, but that is a hunt for a different day."

"Yes, Father." Roger recalled her drawing, and the children crowded around her. "She did give me an idea. If we are to become a learned people again, our children must be taught more than the simple following of customs."

"Yes?" The King leaned forward.

"She had a crowd of children around her learning to draw by watching. If we had someone in the market who could attract the people and teach without them realizing they learn…" Roger trailed off. Put into words the idea sounded fantastical.

"Hmm." His father rubbed his chin. "Interesting notion, and it would help keep the brats from becoming thieves and beggars. Perhaps a storyteller at first, then a scribe. I'll put Tzoca on it. It's the kind of thing he would enjoy overseeing." He roared with laughter and pointed at Roger. "Your face, it looks like someone slapped you with an eel. Don't think I'm not aware of the value of what you learned in Anglia, but you needed to think about it as a Congu, not an Anglian. Your captain sounds like she started you off in the right direction."

"When she returns to port, I will endeavour to introduce her to you." Roger shook on his chair. Why had he thought his father less than wise?

"Do that." The king looked over Roger's shoulder. "Ah, the tea is here, excellent. Set it there." Voz'ci placed the little table where the King indicated, then stepped back.

"You started to tell me of this oath, but we were distracted by a side trail. The oath."

"For some rudeness toward the captain, I promised to help the first person who asked me, regardless of station. I thought it would involve some minor task, an amusing aside."

"A dangerous promise." The King glowered at him. "What if the person had asked for help in overthrowing your father?"

"I would have ordered Chiza to slay me, to prevent dishonour falling on you."

Some deep emotion moved across the King's face, too quickly for Roger to identify it.

"I would ask you refrain from promises which might end in your death." His father's voice spoke evenly, but thunder rolled beneath the words.

"I will try." Roger closed his eyes. "The woman who called in my oath, all unknowing, asked me to do whatever was in my power to stop the raiding across the Sombu river. The young men have started to carry guns, and people are dying unmarked."

"I see." The King closed his eyes and shook his head. "You will need to travel to Mtuaka's domain, and possibly to Sombi. Neither of those places are safe for a Congu prince. Mtuaka blames you for your friend's oathbreaking. How *is* your friend?" The King's eyes bit into Roger.

"He is well, serving on an Anglian steamship."

"One captained by a certain woman?"

"Yes, Father." Roger drew breath to explain further.

"I was told of your conversation with the captain. Her ship is a tiny floating piece of Anglia. It is not something I'd considered, but it might be useful to have a floating bit of Congu someday. You acted correctly, but Mtuaka may feel differently. Be wary around him."

Roger heaved a sigh and willed his heart to beat slower. Cal's determined face popped into his mind. *I need to live up to what she thinks of me.*

"Now, to your oath. I'm thinking it would be useful to open a conversation with King Vvatha, if the foreigners are enticing us, they will be trying to bewitch the Sombi. They may be our enemies, but they have been honourable ones. I would not wish to see them succumb to the cotus flower. You will travel as my herald. You will wear white and carry no weapons. Vvatha is a stubborn and proud man, but I doubt he will kill a herald out of hand. Choose your words carefully, as herald, you speak with my voice." The King stood and walked down the steps. "Do you understand? If you make a promise, I am honour bound to keep it."

"I hear you, Father."

The King strode over to Voz'ci, then circled him. He stood without moving, though Roger saw sweat dripping down his forehead.

"Chiza is well known, and the Sombi might have refused him permission to follow as your right arm. This young man..." The King circled Voz'ci again. "I approve, he will travel with you." He returned to stand before Roger.

"Pour the tea."

Roger poured tea into each cup until nothing else came from the pot.

"Drinking this cup will bind you to your task. Failure will not be punished; betrayal will mean death."

Roger picked up his cup and drained it completely, then placed it upside down in front of him. His father did the same thing.

"Mtuaka arrives in tomorrow. He will hear about your conversation with your captain. Don't be here."

"I hear and obey." Roger stood. The tea ran through his veins setting his whole being to tingling. He bowed and walked out of the hall.

In his sleeping room, he put together a bundle to carry on the road and handed it to Voz'ci.

"Hold onto my knife too." Roger passed it to him. "As my right arm, you may carry weapons to defend me. I have a feeling carrying your father's blade will be useful. I will return shortly. Gather what you need to travel light. We leave as soon as I return."

Roger didn't wait for an answer. He headed toward the baths, where he scrubbed himself from head to toe, leaving only the spot of blood on his forehead. A young servant boy brought him a bundle of clothing, all in white.

"Roger." Bhansin walked into the bath as Roger dressed in the white. "I know you think your brother and I disdain you for your youth and weakness." He put his hand on Roger's shoulder. "That is far from the truth. You walk a different hunt, one we don't understand, but never think we doubt your courage." The First Prince put a thong over Roger's head. "A tooth from the lion which was my first hunt. You are worthy of it."

Roger didn't have a clue what to say, and his throat closed up making words impossible anyway.

Bhansin didn't seem to expect words. Instead he pulled Roger close for an instant, then turned and left. Tcoza met Roger in the hallway.

"Father has sent you away, yet you have an oath to fill here. I will take on your oath and protect who you wish protected."

"Her name is Ilathia." Roger whispered. "Chiza will be with her. She looks like a Sombi, many will not look past her face."

"I will welcome her in your place." Tzoca thumped his chest with his fist. "Good hunting, my brother."

Roger clasped Tozca's arm.

"I will sleep well knowing you will be watching over her." He walked back to his room, crooked his finger at Voz'ci and continued down the hall. The young man carried a large bundle, but had it settled well on his back.

The warriors at the gate saluted them as they left taking the road which would carry them north toward the border.

Chapter 4 Beginnings

Llathia hugged her mother, then picked up the small bundle which was all the belongings she planned to bring to the Staal. Her father had briefly stuck his head out the door and asked her to pick up bread on her way home.

She fought tears back, and for the first time in five years, she walked through the gates to the outside. Chiza walked behind her and slightly to one side.

"Don't stop, don't talk, don't run." He'd told her last night, making her squeak in surprise. She thought he was mute. "I talk to the person I am guarding, any more would be a distraction."

They strolled through the quiet streets, the people who were most likely to cause trouble were most likely sleeping off last night's drinking. A few women sweeping sections of the sidewalk gave her a sharp look, but it held more of pity than anger. At the bottom of the hill, llathia heaved a sigh of relief. She stretched her shoulders, moved the bundle to her other hand and started up the hill.

"Hey, where're you going?" A man stumbled out of a storefront to confront llathia.

"I'm called to the Staal." Llathia winced, she'd just broken two of Chiza's rules. She wouldn't break the third one. Trying to step around the man only made him step in front of her.

"Yeah, sure and I'm the King." The man turned red and pointed down the hill. "Get yourself back to where you belong you—"

Chiza's hand around his throat cut off the rest of the man's words. He pulled uselessly at Chiza's fingers and kicked, but the huge man didn't look away from his victim. Chiza pointed up the hill, and llathia started on her way again. Chiza caught up to her within a few dozen steps.

"Did you...?" llathia couldn't bring herself to finish the question. He gave a miniscule shake of his head. More people were coming out of their homes and stores to stare at them, but Chiza placed himself between her and the onlookers.

Outside the Staal, a man in traditional warrior garb waited for them. He stepped forward and Ilathia braced herself to explain why she'd come.

"I am Tzoca, Second Prince. My brother has been sent away on the King's business. If you need anything, I am at your service." He saluted her with his fist on her chest. Ilathia stared trying desperately to think of something to say.

"I'm not that frightening, am I?" Tzoca smiled at her. "Come Chiza, I'll show her to her room, then we can look at what she needs to get started."

She looked at the big man, he nodded slightly.

"Thank you, my Prince." She tried to return his salute, but her hands got tangled in her straps of her bundle. Heat travelled up her face, but the prince waved for her to follow him as if she'd greeted him flawlessly.

They walked through a bewildering maze of hallways until the prince stopped in front of a room. He knocked on the door and a young woman, maybe even younger than Ilathia, stepped out and knelt before him.

"Thasi, here is the guest I told you about. Serve her faithfully, when she is ready, bring her to me. I'll be in my Kraal." The second prince saluted Ilathia again. "Until later then." He left her alone with Thasi and Chiza.

"Chiza, wait out here." Thasi smiled at him. "Come on, the prince told me you were coming. I have your room prepared." She pulled Ilathia through the curtain. "Here is your reception room. It is allowable for you to greet a male guest here if either Chiza or I am present. If we aren't let them wait in the hallway until we get here. Don't go to talk in the hallway." Thasi pushed aside another curtain. "Here is where we will sleep. I'll be in the corner over there."

"You will sleep here?" Ilathia's voice trembled. She'd never shared a room.

"It is custom. An unmarried woman should not be left alone. It is from the old days when men might abduct a girl to make her his wife."

"Not such old days." Llathia said. "It is still common practice where my parents came from."

"If anyone tries, scream loudly, claw, scratch, bite. They will not last long. This is the King's Staal and you are his guest."

"The King's guest?" Ilathia sat down abruptly on the sleeping mat. "Roger invited me."

"The Third Prince acts with his father's knowledge and blessing. The Second Prince too. You will be safe here."

"Thank you, Thasi." Llathia willed her hands to stop shaking. "I haven't been outside of my home in five years for fear men would see me and assume I was…" The face of the man outside the store flashed into her mind.

"The Second Prince spoke to the King's storesmaster. Everyone knows who you are and why you are here. If anyone is less than courteous, Chiza will deal with them."

Llathia imagined a line of servants lying unconscious behind her and giggled.

"That's better." Thasi pulled aside another curtain. "I didn't know what size you were. The Third Prince didn't say before he left. I have a selection of clothes here. Try on what you would like. Anything you want to keep push to the right. I'll take care of the rest." She lifted a green sheath from the closet. "This would look good with your colouring and your bones. No one said you'd be beautiful. It will make things easier, mostly."

Thasi bullied llathia into trying on the green sheath and a few others too, by the time they were done, llathia had relaxed and giggled along with the young woman.

"For the work I'm doing, I'll need something I can move easily in and won't hurt by getting dirty."

"If I'm not insulting you by the suggestion," Thasi said slowly, "you might be best with something like what I'm wearing. We can put something on it to mark you as a guest."

"That would be perfect." Llathia grinned. "Though I expect to be greasy enough that no one would want me serving them."

"Really?" Thasi raised her eyebrows. "Sounds like fun." She pulled yet another curtain aside to reveal a basin and pitcher. "If you wish to wash, I can help you. Later I will show you to the Staal's baths. There will also be bread and fruit here." Doors revealed a bowl with fruit and a plate with a loaf of bread. A knife lay beside the loaf. Llathia thought of her mother's bread and her stomach rumbled. She cut a slice of the loaf and ate it. It was almost as good as her mother's.

"We shouldn't keep the Second Prince waiting." Llathia brushed crumbs from her fingers and considered the clothes she wore. It would do, though she had no idea what a prince would expect her to wear.

"Let's go, then." Thasi led her out to the hall and away. Llathia jogged to catch up. Chiza moved behind her. He made no sound, but somehow his presence warmed her. They left through the same gate she'd come in through. The warriors saluted her as she passed.

"The princes have their own residences." Thasi explained as she walked. "They are here a lot of course, but they have responsibilities beyond standing with the King. Most of the time they are away. I never saw so much of them until the Third Prince came home." She rolled her eyes. "That was interesting times."

Llathia chanced a look over her shoulder at Chiza. He matched Thasi's eye roll and llathia giggled again.

No one bothered them as they walked. A few people pointed to them. One or two saluted as they passed.

"Everyone around here knows Chiza. If he is acting as your right arm, you must be someone of importance. They can always insult you later, but they can't take back an insult spoken in ignorance."

Thasi ducked into a dim alley. Unlike the ones they'd walked past down the hill, this one was clean, and wide enough for her and Thasi to walk side by side. It led to a gate. Thasi banged on the gate, and it opened wide. A warrior saluted as they walked in.

A woman stepped out of the building on the other side of the courtyard.

"This way." She turned and led them into the house. They found the Prince sitting at a desk talking with several men ranging in age from elderly to young.

"Start off with the most exciting tales. Stories to catch the children's interest. Don't worry if they don't immediately give you full attention. This is a long hunt. Once they come to listen, tell the stories which highlight the need for knowledge beyond jungle tracks. Wait for them to ask you about it, then we'll arrange for a scribe to happen by to teach."

"Yes, my Prince." The men chorused, then left, absently saluting llathia as they passed.

"Ah, llathia." The prince stood and smiled. "Good timing. I was ready to have some tea. Won't you join me?"

"Of course, my Prince." Llathia saluted him.

"Save that for formal occasions." The prince shrugged and waved a hand. "Otherwise we might never get anything done. I am Tzoca. Unless we are in court, or among strangers, that will be enough.

"Yes, my…Tzoca." The prince's name tasted strange in her mouth. Llathia followed him to another room where a man poured water from a kettle into a pot before setting it on the table in front of llathia. He set out cups for her and the prince. Thasi knelt in a corner. Chiza stood like a statue in another.

"I have to confess, for all my concern about keeping Congu traditions, I have a weakness for Zithayan tea." Tzoca settled in on one side of the low table and waved for her to sit. Llathia knelt comfortably.

Tzoca picked up the pot and swirled it gently a few times before pouring tea into the cups. He pushed one to llathia and waited. She picked up the cup and blew gently on the tea before taking a careful sip.

"This is very good." Llathia took another sip. "A mix of bitter and sweet."

"It is one of my favourites, but," Tozca lifted his own cup, "if I start ranting about tea, we will never accomplish anything."

"Some day when we have time, I would like to hear what you have to say." Llathia let the warmth from the cup relax the tightness in her stomach.

Tzoca grinned, and for an instant looked as young as Voz'ci.

"What do you need to teach?"

"I plan to build an engine." Llathia hoped she wouldn't disappoint. "I have worked on every part of my father's engine and listened to him tell the stories of how he built it. The best way to test my knowledge and pass it on is to build a new one."

"Very good." Tzoca sipped at his tea. "Where do we start?"

"First I need a hollow tree. A bottle tree, the shape is best. We bring it here and clean it out, plug it top and bottom. We'll need a lot of rope and pitch for glue. We put the tree on a flat stone and build a furnace beneath it. If we are careful, we can boil the water for steam without lighting the wood on fire."

"Do you want to inspect the trees yourself?"

"It would be best." Llathia shivered and drank more tea. "It would save time. Father's pistons, what the steam moved through to make the engine work, were all different sizes. Not by much, but they too were hollow trunks and he had to work with what he found."

"And you are suggesting we work with something which can be shaped to need." Tzoca tapped his fingers on a table. "Perhaps our bladesmith will have an idea. He's set up at Bhansin's Kraal, we can go see him tomorrow." He looked up at her. "Or do you want the bottle tree first?"

"If he knows what is needed, he can think about it while we search for the right tree."

"Perfect. Tomorrow we see the bladesmith, I'll talk to some foresters and let you know when they are ready for you."

"Thank you, Tzoca." Llathia liked the spark of enthusiasm in his eyes. He looked like the Third Prince's brother in that moment. "If I may ask an impertinent question?" She held her breath but Tzoca waved for her to continue. "Chiza was the Third Prince's right arm. But I don't see one following you…"

Tzoca laughed. "Bura is close, but I'm more recognizable than Roger, him just having returned from Anglia. The arm may choose invisibility as a better response than presence. Be assured if I walk outside these walls, or the walls of my brother's Kraal or father's Staal, he is very much present. You'll meet him tomorrow."

"One last thing." Llathia finished her tea and reluctantly put her empty cup on the table. "If I might have paper and charcoal, I will try to draw the machine to help explain it to others."

"I have just the thing." Tzoca stood gracefully. "Wait here for me. Pour yourself another cup if you like."

Llathia swirled the pot and poured more tea. It came out darker, and tasted more bitter, but still a flavour to be enjoyed. Tzoca returned with a roll of paper and another roll made of leather.

"These are pencils I bought from a trader, mostly as a curiosity. If you can use them, please." He handed the rolls to her and bowed slightly.

Llathia stood and hefted the rolls, but Thasi took them from her with a grin.

"Thank you, Tzoca." Llathia smiled. "Thank you for the tea."

Thasi chattered on the way home about how much she enjoyed serving the Second Prince, and how she looked forward to serving llathia. Llathia let the words flow over her and remembered Tzoca's smile and joy over his tea. She shook herself. *Don't be foolish, girl. He's a prince for all you call him by name. Don't forget it.*

Chapter 5 First Steps

Roger walked with Voz'ci through the night jungle. Noises let them know all was well as they passed. When toward dawn, the noises stopped. Voz'ci put his hand on Roger's shoulder.

"Someone's up ahead. From what your father said, it could be Mtuaka."

"Probably." Roger pushed the bile down. He couldn't honourably challenge the man, though he was as vile as they come. For all that he had to support Mtuaka against Bundo, his heart rejoiced to know a young girl had been freed from this man's harem. "We will leave the trail and rest until they have passed." They slipped through the thick brush into the more open jungle. Voz'ci led them half an hour before he found a large boulder which pushed up through the forest floor. On one side a sandy spot made a good place to rest.

"I will keep watch." Voz'ci vanished into the jungle. Roger nodded his head, the young man hadn't forgotten his hunt, though he lived in the city.

The light grew as the sun rose above the canopy. Day sounds replaced those of the night. He listened to the familiar chorus. When it ceased, he stiffened, then stood.

"Should have known it would be the Anglian prince." A man, almost as tall as Chiza swaggered into the clearing and looked Roger up and down. Where Chiza held a well-hidden strength, this man exuded brute force. The intruder's lips curled in contempt.

"I am on a mission for my father as a herald." Roger met Ntoox's eyes.

"Or you wear white because you are too cowardly to fight." Ntoox reached for his knife. "No one will find you here alone in the jungle, many heralds never return."

A knife planted itself in the ground between the two of them.

"Not quite alone." Roger said.

Ntoox spat and retreated into the jungle. After a long time, the sounds of the animals returned. Voz'ci dropped out of a tree and picked up his knife.

"You did well." Roger grinned at the young man. "He expected Chiza, the only person aside from my father he fears."

"He walks like his first hunt was a cow." Voz'ci snorted. "Who is he?"

"Ntoox, Mtuaka's heir, the son of his sister. For all he has the largest harem in Congu, Mtuaka has no heir of his own."

"Good thing he's going in the opposite direction."

"For now." Roger rolled his head to loosen the tension still in his shoulders. "There will come a day when we settle our dispute."

"I admire you more for having an enemy like that." Voz'ci picked up the bundle. "If we travel this way, there is a stream and I could use a drink."

***

llathia woke in the dark and heard someone breathing in her room. Her heart raced until a name came to her. *Thasi.* She hadn't told llathia what to do if she woke in the night needing a pot. As if thinking of her need wakened the young woman, Thasi woke.

"Mistress, how may I aid you?"

"I, uh.." llathia's face heated.

A light blossomed showing Thasi frowning, holding a shielded lamp.

"My deepest apologies, mistress. My neglect has embarrassed you. Come, I will take you to the baths."

They padded on bare feet down the dark hallway to where Thasi lifted a curtain for llathia, then followed her in.

"To your left, there is a curtain. Beyond is what you need. Call if you desire assistance."

Llathia pushed through into the tiny room. Cubicles lined one wall. In one she did what she needed and sighed in relief. A chain hung on the wall beside her. Curious, she gave it a tug. Water splashed from an opening in the wall. Llathia rinsed her hands and the rest went down the hole. Out in the cubicle a small table held towels. She dried her hands, then dropped the towel in a basket with others.

Thasi bowed deeply.

"It is my work to be with you. Whenever you have need, no matter the time of night, speak my name and I will answer."

"Thasi, this is all new to me." Llathia turned to examine what she could of the room in the light of the tiny lantern. "Did you say this was the baths? I don't think I can get back to sleep easily."

"Come this way." Thasi led her to where a pool of water took up most of the floor. "Let me wash you before you enter." She took llathia's nightshirt and llathia hardly registered her words. "You are safe." Thasi wrapped a towel around llathia. "Not all are comfortable with being unclothed, even here. If you allow, I won't wear a towel, it makes it harder to wash you properly."

She took Ilathia's hand and pulled her over to the side where another chain dangled. A stool rested below a spout. Thasi took the towel as Llathia sat and braced herself for a torrent of water. When Thasi pulled the chain, a gentle flow streamed over her, refreshing and rejuvenating.

The water stopped and Thasi's hands rubbed soap over her and massaged it into her hair. It made her feel young again, her mother bathing her in a wood tub and singing to her in a language Ilathia guessed to be Sombi. She hummed the tune.

"What is that, mistress?" Thasi paused.

"Something my mother sang to me when I was a child." Ilathia shook with the need for her mother's touch. She'd never left their home and now, she was here in a strange place being washed by a stranger in the middle of the night. Her breaths came in gasps.

"It is hard, leaving home." Thasi's voice came as a whisper. "When I began working in the Second Prince's Kraal, I cried myself to sleep. Only knowing I'd dishonour my family kept me there. Once a year, the prince sends me home to see them. I smile and give them gifts and tell them stories of life in the prince's house, knowing when I return to the Kraal, I will cry myself to sleep again for days after. The Second Prince is kind and understands."

"What did you do in the prince's home?" Ilathia pushed her thoughts away from thinking of Thasi washing the prince.

"I cleaned the rooms, I served his guests. He is an honourable master. He has said when I am ready, he will allow me to marry. There is this warrior in the First Princes Kraal..." Thasi's hands paused.

"Maybe we will see him tomorrow and you can point him out to me." Llathia said. "There is a young man who visited us more often than anyone else. He likes to look at me. I don't dislike him, but I'm not sure what it would feel like to like him, as you do your warrior."

Thasi's hands took up massaging llathia's hair again, then pulled the chain sending another cascade over llathia.

"Come on." Thasi pulled llathia to her feet. She couldn't help but compare the young woman's muscular full body with her own bony figure. They sat on the edge of the pool then slipped in. Thasi sighed. "This is so much nicer than the one at the Second Prince's Kraal."

"You've used the prince's bath?" llathia had to fight off visions of the prince again.

Thasi laughed. "No, the servants have their own, one for men and one for women. There is another for women guests, and the Prince uses the last and shares with any male guests. Not that we've had a lot of guests of any description lately."

They rested comfortably in the water which was warmer than llathia had expected.

"It is stored in a tank on the roof. The King bought a boiler from a ship that was being scrapped. The sun heats it." Thasi dunked her head then shook the water from her hair, which hung in countless braids to rest on her shoulders. Llathia followed suit, though her hair was more like the moss which grew on the fence in places. Short and tight to her scalp.

"Mistress, you are beautiful." Thasi stared at her with wide eyes. "You look like a Queen." She ducked her head as her face darkened.

"Thasi," llathia put her finger under the young woman's chin and lifted it. "I need a friend more than I need a servant. Let us be friends when we are alone. You may call me mistress when there are ears to hear it."

"But you are royal. The Second Prince himself told me to treat you like a princess."

Llathia laughed until it echoed off the walls and she put her hand over her mouth in fear of waking the Staal.

"I am no princess. My father built an engine from what he saw when he worked on a steamship many years ago. He and my mother are from near the Sombu River, and there is as much Sombi in them as Congu. Mother tells me I look like a Sombi from the Biafa on the Lower Sea. That is why I couldn't go out. Where I live, there is only one occupation for a woman who looks the least bit Sombi."

"Then why?" Thasi's eyes were wide as her mouth dropped open.

"I plan to build the King an engine like my father's. That is my hunt."

"Mistress," Thasi tried to bow and splashed her face into the water. "Whatever I may do to help, I will." She pouted a little. "I always wanted to serve a princess."

"Well, if it makes you feel better, you may pretend I'm a princess." Thasi looked so delighted that Ilathia splashed her. "Just wait until you are scrubbing grease from my hair."

Thasi laughed and then they rested quietly until Ilathia pulled herself reluctantly from the pool. Thasi lifted herself gracefully out, then used a towel to dry Ilathia. She helped Ilathia into her nightdress, then dried herself and put her garment on.

Outside in the hall, Chiza waited, still as if he were part of the wall.

"Sorry to wake you," Ilathia said. He responded with the slightest of head shakes.

Back in her room, Thasi fussed to make sure she was comfortable.

"Are all right arms like Chiza?" Ilathia rested her head on the pillow.

"If you mean, do they all do that silent thing, yes. But Chiza is a legend. He was the King's own right arm before he was sent with the Third Prince to Anglia. There is not a warrior in the country who can touch him." She brushed her fingers across llathia's brow. "Sleep well, my princess."

***

In the morning, Thasi woke llathia holding a plate of fruit cut into pieces. Llathia sat cross legged on her bed and nibbled at them while Thasi went through the clothes choosing what she thought llathia should wear.

Once dressed, llathia sighed. At least it was easy to walk in, but it wouldn't do at all for serious work.

"Remember, I will need some plain, comfortable clothes to work in. Maybe put a pin on them so I don't get mistaken for a servant, though with Chiza standing behind me, it isn't likely to happen."

Thasi giggled and nodded. "I will let them know. Wait here for me." She bustled out of the room. Llathia moved into the front room.

"Chiza, is it ok if we talk?"

He stepped into the room and saluted her.

"What do you need, mistress?"

"What do you call the Third Prince in private?" llathia put her hands on her hips.

"Roger, or occasionally, damned fool." Chiza grinned briefly and llathia caught a glimpse of an entirely different man.

"So, you will call me llathia, or damned fool, if the circumstances warrant." Llathia fixed him with a stare until he nodded.

"I know nothing of living with royalty. I'm more comfortable in men's clothing, covered with grease from head to toe. I don't want to embarrass the Second Prince, the King, or anyone else."

"Trust Thasi. If the Second Prince sent her to you, she is more than she appears. She will be trained to talk to everyone from the King himself to the beggar at the gate. If in doubt, let her speak for you. I am your right arm. It is my place to protect you. Unfortunately, that doesn't leave time for giving advice."

"Is life here so dangerous?" Ilathia wrapped her around herself.

"It can be." Chiza sighed. "At any time, a tribal lord may decide he would be a better King. Attacks on the princes are not unheard of. You are valuable because of your knowledge. If you were removed it would embarrass the King and set back his desire to move Congu forward."

"But I haven't done anything yet."

"You will."

Thasi appeared.

"All set, they will replace the clothes with things which will fit you. I had to argue hard to get you your work clothes."

"Thank you, Thasi." Llathia braced herself. "Let's not keep the Second Prince waiting."

They headed off along the hall, Thasi leading with an unerring knowledge of the Staal.

"The King is welcoming guests." She whispered, so I'm taking a longer way around to avoid them."

They arrived at the gate without incident. The Second Prince stood talking with one of the warriors at the gate. A man without Chiza's size, but the same ruthless stillness loomed behind the prince.

"Ah there you are." The Second Prince smiled at Ilathia. "That colour looks good on you." He headed off into the city before Ilathia could come up with a reply. Thasi had a smug look on her face.

They walked along a level road until it bent and Ilathia gasped at the view. She could see all the way to the ocean gleaming turquoise as far as the horizon.

"It is quite a sight." Tzoca stood beside her. "I'm the traditionalist of the family. My Kraal is built to be easily defended, because that's how it was done, not because it is needed. I argued against Roger going away to school, I was annoyed when he came home with his ideas about how to change everything." He sighed. "My father has trusted me with the work of ensuring we don't lose ourselves in the change that is already happening. How am I supposed to do that?"

"What is the heart of being Congu?" Ilathia asked. "Protect that."

"Wise words. I thank you." Tzoca saluted her without the slightest irony. He headed along the road, Ilathia followed with Thasi, Chiza and Bura bringing up the rear.

The First Prince's Kraal stood in the centre of a wide courtyard. Warriors stood like statues around it.

"My brother doesn't like closed in spaces." Tzoca's lips twisted a little.

The First Prince walked out to greet them.

"I hear you are the engine-smith." He ran his eyes over Ilathia, like he might assess a new warrior. "If I may aid you, call on me and my household."

"If I may speak to the bladesmith?" Ilathia said, then blushed at leaving off the honorifics.

"This way." He turned and walked around to the back of the house. "Tzoca, you didn't tell me she was such a beauty."

"She is?" Tzoca turned and looked at her like he was seeing her for the first time. His brother slapped Tzoca's head. "Tell me what you *did* notice about her."

"She likes tea, and she told me I was to find the heart of being Congu and protect that."

"You'll have to introduce her to father."

Llathia's heart raced at the idea of meeting the King.

"Not until Mtuaka has left. I don't want any trouble. I should have put her up at my Kraal, or yours."

"She has Chiza as her right arm. Even Mtuaka knows better than to trouble him."

"I hope so. I heard Ntoox came with him."

"He's trouble. I know he's related by blood, but Mtuaka would be better choosing an heir with some subtlety."

Llathia wrapped her arms around herself. Who was this man who worried the princes? She glanced over at Thasi, whose lips were thinned, then forgot her concern at the sound of hammering.

"There." The First Prince pointed. "I would love to stay, but father has asked me to attend him today."

"Carry a sharp knife." Tzoca said.

They followed the sound of the hammer until they found a man with one leg wearing only a waist wrap, banging a glowing piece of something with a hammer. The colour faded from bright orange to dull red as llathia watched.

"Pardon, my prince." The man set the piece and the hammer aside and hopped around to face them. "How may I help you?"

"This is llathia, our engine-smith."

"I'm Bh'ob." The bladesmith saluted her. "Voz'ci talked a lot about you from his visits down the hill. I'm sure he would have made up excuses to go, but I needed him around the shop, and he's learning the trade." Bh'ob looked over at the prince. "Pardon, but do you have word of my son? I expected him to return last night."

"The King has sent him on a hunt with the Third Prince."

Bh'ob wiped his face with a cloth. "Sounds like Voz'ci. I will have to find someone to help out while he's gone." He sighed and nodded at Ilathia. "Don't want to sound cold, but Voz'ci wanted a hunt more even than to visit your father."

"I'm sure he will do well."

Bh'ob nodded, then shook his head.

"What do you need from me?"

"I'm going to need tubes, about so big." She held her hands apart. "They must be able to handle pressure. At least two, more if you can."

Bh'ob pointed at the piece he had been shaping with the hammer. "I've been working on that all morning. I can't imagine how I'd build what you want." He scratched his head. There are people I can ask. How long would you want these tubes?"

"At least the height of Chiza." She pointed back at him.

"Please don't tell me you need them in a hurry."

"I need them done right more than I need them fast."

Bh'ob nodded again. Then picked up his hammer. "If you'll pardon me, I'd like to finish this blade before I head downhill to see the old men."

"Thank you for your time." Llathia saluted, but he'd already put the piece in the fire and was working a handle. The coals burned bright.

"Come." Tzoca put his hand on her shoulder briefly. "We need to get back. I expect father will be calling for me, and I need to find someone to send to help the bladesmith."

They walked back along the road in silence. Llathia tried to think of what she needed to do next. "Tzoca," she covered her mouth, but he only turned to her and raised his eyebrow. "I will need helpers. Ones who won't mind getting dirty and doing things that don't make sense to anyone."

"How many?"

"I don't know yet." Llathia paused at the place with the view and leaned on the wall. "It is more than just building the thing. They need to be willing to learn how to make one themselves. Make it stronger, safer."

"Safer?"

"There are powerful forces involved, a mistake could be catastrophic. We should work somewhere far from people."

"Surely you're exaggerating." Tzoca pointed down at a ship tied to dock, a thin string of smoke coming from the stack. "They have engines on their—"

A puff of smoke caught llathia's eye, then the sound arrived as a physical blow.

"What?" Tzoca pulled her back as Chiza and Bura stepped forward.

"It came from the bottom, over there." Chiza paused and turned to face llathia. "The smoke is rising from your father's yard."

Llathia' heart felt like a spear had gone through it. She was barely aware of Chiza catching her before she could climb over the wall.

"I will send men down immediately." Tzoca put a hand on her arm. Bura had already vanished down the road.

"Let's get her to the Staal." Thasi shook her head. "Poor girl."

Arms cradled her as llathia gave herself over to her grief.

Chapter 6 Troubled Hunt

Roger and Voz'ci made good time once they returned to the trail. Roger worried about Ntoox. The man was a brute, but even he should have thought twice about attacking a herald. By tradition, killing a herald brought a curse on the killer's head. Tradition looked to be failing. Tzoca was right. The Congu were losing their way.

The air grew thicker as they worked their way inland. Their clothes were damp, not from sweat but from the moisture in the air. The temperature dropped, slowly chilling him. Walking helped keep him warm.

Voz'ci had started off hyper-alert, starting at every strange sound. Now he'd become more like Chiza, aware, but not reacting to anything unnecessary. They went past the trail leading to Mtuaka's Staal. Roger had never been up this way. All his hunting had been on the high plains to the south.

They arrived at a village, and the headsman came out to welcome them.

"We have no guest room, but you are welcome to my bed."

Roger caught a whiff of the man.

"I must camp alone." He waved at his white clothing, or at least mostly white. He'd picked up a few stains as they travelled.

Voz'ci set up a lean-to a few minutes out of the village. They rested while Roger contemplated about his next move. He didn't think baldly asking about the raids would be very effective. When the headsman came out, he hadn't seen many young warriors. Either they had hidden to ambush trouble, or they weren't at home.

The following day, Roger returned to the village and wandered around. As he'd thought, there weren't many young warriors. The few which were there had sullen faces, all of them turned their backs and avoided Roger. He wasn't ready to try to force them to give him answers.

In line with his refusal of a bed, Roger declined half-hearted offers of food from the women. They appeared more relieved than disappointed when he left them to go back to the jungle.

He found some roots and greens while Voz'ci caught small game for them to roast.

"Did you notice," Voz'ci scrubbed at the grease on his chin, "there wasn't any meat cooking? This close to a village I expected a harder time finding game."

"They must have found a different hunt. We will travel on tomorrow. I want to get to the river."

Voz'ci nodded, then cocked his head.

"Trouble." He slid into the brush leaving Roger to finish his meal alone.

The young man returned in a short time.

"You'd better come see this." Voz'ci walked ahead of Roger, on his toes, hand near his knife.

In the village, a woman wailed over a body lying in the dirt. Others cried off to the side. Young men stalked about brimming with rage, swearing and slashing at the jungle.

"You aren't wanted here." One of them snarled at Roger as he stepped out into the clearing.

"What do you imagine the King's response to interfering with his herald would be?" Roger pushed past the warrior. A thud behind him suggested Voz'ci had been more forceful.

The dead man had a hole in his stomach. It looked hardly larger than an arrow would make.

"Turn him over." Roger hardly recognized the cold voice coming from his mouth. Resentfully the warriors flipped the corpse over. The hole in his back was big enough for Roger to put his fist in. He'd seen bullet wounds in Anglia. A hunting accident, from the grief on the faces of the people around him, he'd believed them. There was no grief on the faces here, not on the warriors.

"Why were you raiding if you knew they had guns?" That strange, cold voice spoke for him again.

"How else would we get our own guns. Mtuaka refuses to give us any."

Roger's hand clenched at the warrior's words, but the young man kept up his complaints.

"Do not throw your lives away." Roger didn't look up from the dead man's back. "If you get guns, do you know how to use them? Do you have ammunition and gun-powder? Without that a gun is a useless stick."

"What do you know of guns?" The warrior jumped to his feet, the others gathering around him.

Roger pulled open his tunic to show the puckered scar where the bullet had pierced his side, missing everything.

"I know." He re-arranged his clothes and stepped forward to stand nose to nose with the young warrior. "Hunt for your families, feed them. That is honour. Dying without ever seeing your enemy…" He shrugged and pointed to the clump of grieving women. "Do they look happy?"

Roger turned and walked out of the village, when he got to their camp. He breathed deeply until he drowned the rage burning in his gut.

"It is a good thing I am not allowed to carry a weapon." Roger said when Voz'ci appeared. "There would have been a bloodbath."

"You left them trembling in fear." Voz'ci said. "Warriors like them will look for someone to blame for their fear. We should leave before they work themselves up enough to hunt you. We'll travel through the jungle for the rest of the day. They won't look off the road."

He packed up his gear and shouldered the bundle. Roger followed him into the jungle.

They walked two days through the jungle, eating well on Voz'ci's hunting.

"You grew up in the city, how is it you are so good in the jungle?" Roger leaned against a tree to rest.

"When my father was sailing about the world, I lived with my grandfather. He lived for the old days. We stalked game and watched predator and prey together. It's in my blood. When father returned missing a leg, grandfather sent me to help and learn. But any day I have off, I head into the jungle to track."

"We need more like you."

"What, old-fashioned?" Voz'ci sighed. "My friends were more interested in girls and trouble than hunting."

"Men who blend the old and the new."

After they rejoined the trail, they only stopped briefly in the villages. Some had few warriors, and mothers with drawn faces. Others buzzed with anger as warriors looked for someone to blame for their failure. Roger saw more bullet wounds. Each time he told them the same thing. He didn't stay around to see if any of them listened. They avoided troops of young men on the trail.

"If that many warriors are raiding, it must be almost a war." Roger pinched his nose. "We haven't seen any Sombi warriors."

"We may learn the reason for that by the river." Voz'ci said. "I would feel better if we stayed off the trail from here. The river is close, but my gut tells me trouble is closer."

They took to following the trail from a bow shot away. A group of men trotted past.

"Let's follow them and see what they're up to." Roger pushed himself into motion. Voz'ci moved easily making Roger feel old.

The warriors slowed and camped for the night. None of them hunted, instead they ate grain porridge.

"How long have they been raiding instead of hunting?" Roger asked softly.

"We counted how many young men were in the villages, but we didn't look for their fathers."

They followed through the next morning until the warriors stopped, then made an attempt at moving silently. Roger and Voz'ci travelled ahead to where the jungle stopped. Figures worked in fields. They looked Congu. Young men walked about carrying rifles. They were Sombi. A walled village lay past the field.

"When did the Sombi begin to claim our land?" Roger peered through the brush, grinding his teeth. Mtuaka should have been doing something about this. But the only thing people said about him was that he wouldn't give them guns. Like he had guns to give away.

"Mtuaka is planning to overthrow father." Roger's gut clenched. "He's got his hands on enough guns he thinks he can do it."

"Your father is a wily hunter."

"Yes, but even the lion is prey if he doesn't know he's being stalked. You must go and warn him."

"Your father would kill me for leaving you." Voz'ci grimaced. "I'd prefer not to die any time soon."

"What then?" Roger wanted to turn and run for home himself.

"What would the King do if warriors started showing up demanding he give them the guns that Mtuaka refuses them?"

"Let's find those idiots." Roger pushed himself back, but Voz'ci's hand pinned him to the jungle floor.

"Too late."

A group of warriors burst out of the jungle and swarmed a Sombi with a rifle. One of them snatched up the weapon and fired a shot at another Sombi. The bullet couldn't have gone anywhere close. The warrior kept pulling on the trigger.

"He has to reload. The Sombi will have cartridges." Roger wanted to close his eyes, but he needed to see this.

The other Sombi pointed toward the group of warriors as some broke off and dashed toward the next closest Sombi. The man coolly aimed his rifle and fired. A Congu went down. He opened the gun, and loaded another cartridge, closed it, fired again. Another man fell in a heap. They looked to be too close for the Sombi to load and fire a third shot. Instead he dropped to the ground. The Congu yelled and jeered. Then shots came from all directions and tore apart the Congu warriors. The Sombi stood and dusted himself off, then shouted at the workers in the fields who had also dropped to the ground.

"Back." Voz'ci said and they retraced their steps.

"Let's see if any of the fools survived." Roger wanted to weep, but his anger wouldn't let him. They came across a young man, hardly more than a boy, shaking and crying on the road.

"Listen." Roger picked the boy up and shook him. "Listen to me." The warrior stank of fear. "Go to the King. Tell him you want guns to fight the Sombi."

"Mtuaka won't give us any."

"Not Mtuaka, the King. Ask him for guns." Roger pushed the boy along the trail. "Run, boy." The warrior started hobbling back along the trail, then he picked up speed until he was sprinting away from them.

"I'm not sure what scared him more, you or the Sombi." Voz'ci shook his head. "I hope he doesn't kill himself before he gets there." He slapped his hands together. "Now what?"

"We go talk to the Sombi." Roger said. "Let's hope they don't shoot us before asking questions."

***

"My Prince." Tashi's voice had an edge of desperation in it. "You may go no further."

"Just to lay her on her bed." Tzoca pleaded.

Why was Tzoca pleading? Wasn't Chiza carrying her? Llathia lifted her head and looked into the Second Prince's pain filled eyes. She pushed away. He shouldn't be carrying her. What if someone saw? Chiza stood where he commanded both the door and the room. His face might have been carved from stone.

"Put me down." Llathia's words tore at her already sore throat. Tzoca gently set her on her feet.

"Why are you carrying me?" Her voice cracked. "You're a Prince."

"Chiza is your Arm. He cannot carry you and protect you." Tzoca stepped back as his face closed. "I will leave you with your maid." He turned and left the room. Thasi took llathia's arm and guided her to her mat.

"What's wrong with Tzoca?" llathia held her head. "Did I say something wrong?"

"Don't worry about it." Thasi sat beside her and stroked her back. "He will forgive you anything."

Something about that felt strange, but llathia had no strength to think about it. Her mind and heart were yawning gulfs.

"Could you get me some tea?" She winced at how weak and whiny she sounded, but Thasi nodded, patted her back and went out of the room. Llathia lay down and let the sobs come again. If she'd stayed with her father, would she have been able to save them? The relief she felt at being alive tore at her.

"Here." A gentle hand shook llathia. "Drink this, it will soothe your throat, then you can sleep more."

The tea warmed her, not like Tozca's, but like gentle embers glided down absorbing the sharp edges of pain. She didn't remember finishing the tea.

***

A gentle tune woke llathia, she kept her eyes closed, unwilling to open them to the cruel world which made her an orphan. A hand ran from her head to the small of her back, as her mother once did. Tears leaked out of her eyes to disappear in an already soaked pillow.

"Come, you can't lie there forever." Her mother's voice chided her. Llathia sat up to rebuke the ghost which tormented her. She looked into her mother's face, tears gliding down the ebony cheeks. Words escaped her, Ilathia threw her arms around her mother, still afraid she'd fade away like a ghost. Solid, strong arms wrapped themselves around Ilathia.

"There, there." Her mother patted Ilathia's back. "I'm sorry to have caused you such grief."

"What?" Ilathia pushed away so she could look her mother in the eyes. "How is it your fault I thought you and father both dead?" Sudden hope bloomed then died when she saw the pain in her mother's face.

"I had gone out to buy flour. When I heard the explosion, I ran home. It was all gone. The entire shed, all his work, vanished in an instant. The fence too, all the lumber he'd cut scattered through the neighbourhood. In all the years he ran his machine, I never dreamed it could end like that."

"He was always balanced on the edge of disaster." Llathia whispered. "I tried to convince him to add some safety valve, but it would mean shutting down, and he couldn't stand the thought. When I build mine, there will be safety valves and other things father talked of but never did."

"Can you do this?" Her mother's hands caressed her cheeks.

"I have to, for father, so his dream doesn't die."

"That's my girl." A twisted smile flickered across her mother's face.

"Oh good, you're up." Thasi entered the room carrying a tray. "The Second Prince's man sent your mother up as soon as they found her. No one else died, but the explosion wrecked a lot of homes."

"Use whatever lumber is salvageable to rebuild." Nnontui said. "It is the least I can do."

"I will send a message to the Second Prince." Thasi set the tray on the floor and slipped out.

Llathia poured tea with a shaky hand, still afraid her mother would vanish. Thasi returned and served cheese and bread.

Nnontui tilted her head as she chewed the bread. "Not bad."

"This is the best bread in the Staal." Thasi leaned back on her heels, and you say it's 'not bad'?"

Llathia laughed, a strange feeling.

"Mother makes the best bread I've ever tasted."

"Hmm." Thasi thought for a moment. "Pardon me, mistress." She stood and left. Llathia shrugged and reached for more bread. Suddenly, she was ravenous.

They'd finished the tray and llathia had raided the food behind the curtain in her room and finished most of it too.

"I can't believe I'm so hungry."

"Well, you did sleep for the better part of two days." Warm eyes glowed over the tea cup her mother held."

"Two days?" llathia froze trying to process the knowledge.

Thasi returned and called them out to the front room. A man waited for them there.

"Thasi tells me you are a baker." The man assessed nnontui.

"I make a decent loaf of bread." Nnontui lowered her head. "And I can turn my hand to a few other things."

"I'm the storesmaster of the Second Prince's Kraal. We recently had our baker leave our kitchen. Thasi has asked me to allow you to try the position."

"You want me to work in a Prince's kitchen?" Nnontui laughed, then stopped when the man's expression didn't change. "You're serious, aren't you? If I work for you, I'll be able to see llathia regularly?"

"Of course." The man looked shocked she needed to ask.

"Then I will work for you." She stood and bowed. "I am nnontui Cjola, widow of Gkuna Cjola, inventor and engine-smith."

"Welcome nnontui." The man didn't look upset at her mother's Sombi name, but Thasi would have told him her name. "When you are ready to come to the Second Prince's Kraal, ask one of the warriors and they will show you the way. If you at any time feel unsafe, a warrior will escort you."

"Thank you." Nnontui saluted him.

The man left and Thasi smiled at them, obviously pleased with herself.

"Thank you, Thasi." Llathia grinned at her. "It will be nice to have my mother close at hand."

"I give you thanks as well." Nnontui saluted. "I will enjoy having employment again, and there is nothing for me down the hill." Sorrow flashed across her face, and Llathia took her hand and squeezed it.

They returned to the safety of the bedroom and chatted until Llathia's mother stretched and sighed.

"I'd better get over to my new home. I don't want to be too slow." She hugged Llathia, then Thasi left to guide her to the front gate.

"Pardon, mistress." A voice called from the front room. Llathia peeked out to see a middle-aged woman in the same clothes as Thasi.

"What can I do for you?" Llathia stepped out into the room.

"The First Wife has asked to meet with you."

Llathia gulped and wished Thasi were here to advise her.

"Let me put someone on more suitable for meeting the First Wife." Llathia thought she caught a slight nod of approval. She almost panicked, looking at the closet. The dresses had multiplied, almost overflowing the space. Her hand wavered over the selection of beautiful colours, then settled on the plain white which looked like a finer version of the servant's uniform. A pin on the breast showed a hand with a knife and another with a needle pulling a dangling thread. Must be the thing to mark her apart from the servants.

She was here as an engine-smith, not a princess. She'd go dressed as such. Llathia splashed water on her face and scrubbed it with a towel. For once she blessed her hair, it never needed any fussing. The white clothes fit perfectly and gave her a confidence she hadn't had with the fancier outfits. *This is who I am.*

The woman's eyes widened slightly when llathia returned, but she didn't say anything. She led llathia through maze of hallways. At one door, two women warriors stood with spears. They frowned at Chiza. He met their gaze for a long moment then stationed himself against the wall, immovable as a mountain.

"Only women are allowed past this door." The woman explained as she pulled llathia through the door. "Even the King himself cannot enter."

The decoration changed from the utilitarian white of the outside corridors to lush fabric hanging from ceiling and walls. Llathia glanced at a painting as she passed and felt heat on her face. She didn't need that image in her mind.

The woman knocked on a door and a female warrior opened it and waved llatthia in.

"I will wait here." The woman nodded at llathia.

The warrior led her into a room hung with gold. Tinkling water suggested a fountain somewhere in the room, but llathia couldn't see it. They walked briskly past tables laden with everything from food to art which made llathia blush more.

Brighter light silhouetted a figure sitting upright in a chair. The warrior walked over to the woman, knelt and saluted. Llathia wasn't sure what to do, so she copied the warrior.

The woman shifted restlessly, but llathia wouldn't move until the warrior did.

"Stand up, dear." The voice was like honey. Llathia stood as the woman flicked her hand dismissing the warrior. "Is this what you wear to meet the First Wife?" The First Wife frowned.

"My apologies, First Wife, but I am here as an engine-smith. This is what I will wear."

"Ah." The First Wife tilted her head and examined llathia from head to toe. Llathia shivered as if she stood naked in front of the woman. "I can see what the gossip is about. Not a First Wife, but something else?"

llathia kept her face still even as she tried to understand what the First Wife was talking about. *First Wife? For who? It's absurd.*

"You have restraint." The First Wife nodded slightly. "I approve." She frowned. "I heard the explosion down the hill was an engine."

"Yes, First Wife, my father's boiler failed."

She waved her hand as if details didn't matter.

"I would be displeased if such an incident were to damage my husband's honour."

"I have already thought of ways to prevent such an explosion. There is danger, so we will work away from others. If it does fail, I will be the first to die."

"You talk like a warrior, about dying." The First Wife's frown deepened.

"You know, First Wife, others beside warriors risk their lives in service of the King."

"Well said." The First Wife's lips twitched. "Take care, your engine may not be the greatest danger to your life."

Llathia wanted to ask what she meant, but a warrior appeared to salute the First Wife, then took Llathia's arm. She saluted and followed the warrior without a word.

The conversation played in her head and refused to settle into any kind of sense. Llathia pushed it out of her mind. Chiza stepped forward as llathia exited the woman's wing of the Staal. He fell in behind as the middle-aged woman guided llathia back to her room.

Thasi paced in the front room. She saluted the other servant, then pulled llathia back into the bedroom.

"You went to see the First Wife in that?" Thasi looked ready to faint.

"I wanted her to think of me as an engine-smith." Llathia tried to recover her reasons, but the First Wife's words tangled in her head.

"Perhaps that's best." Thasi sighed and dropped onto her mat. "I about died when I returned, and you weren't here. To learn you'd been taken to the First Wife only made it worse."

"Maybe she waited until you were gone," Llathia said. "It seems like the kind of thing she would do."

Thasi laughed and relaxed.

"You're right, but don't even hint at that outside this room. She is a bad enemy."

"I guessed that." Llathia dropped sat on the floor. "I don't know if I've ever been that scared or confused. It was like we were having two different conversations."

"I've heard she's like that. The First Wife has the sharpest political mind in Congu."

"Is there a Second Wife?"

Thasi looked around as if someone might be listening.

"It's the only time the King didn't heed the First Wife. There was a rumour, the Second Wife had bewitched the King, but First Wife put an end to that. They are polite, Third Prince is Second Wife's son. So in the Hcazo tribe, he is First Prince, but he has refused clan leadership. His cousin is The Hcazo, and by all measures is doing a good job, but they are a tiny tribe with little influence."

"Right." Llathia tried to assemble the pieces in her head, but too many were missing. "She did express concern over the safety of the engine, given the explosion. I assured her I had plans to prevent a repeat, and I would be first to die if it did fail. She told me I talked like a warrior. Don't know if she meant it as a compliment."

"Warriors are necessary but shouldn't run the tribe. First Wife would not accept a situation where she needed to die, because she is too important to the Congu."

"She is First Wife." Llathia said. "Why would she be in danger?"

Thasi shook her head and sighed.

"Remember there is only one of you. If you die, we lose the engine and all that it means. Don't rush to sacrifice yourself."

"Maybe that's what she meant." Llathia rubbed her temples trying to think. "In that case, I understand."

"Good." Thasi smiled. "Tomorrow we go looking for your tree."

"Tomorrow?" llathia closed her eyes. The wounds in her heart were still fresh, hardly scabbed over, but sitting around wouldn't help. "I'll be ready. Where did you put the paper and pencils, the Second Prince gave me? I'd like to try to draw out what I need."

Thasi fetched them from a cubby hole. Llathia's heart twinged as she unrolled the fine leather and saw the selection of pencils. *How could he just give this to me? But then he's a Prince, it's just a thing to him.*

Llathia struggled to put her vision on paper.

"I wish I knew how to draw better." She thickened a line to define a shape better. "I need to figure out how to make a safety valve. How to have something only open at a certain pressure?" Thasi looked over her shoulder but didn't say anything.

Chapter 7 Baited Net

"Before you walk out there, change your clothes." Voz'ci opened his bundle and pulled out a set of white clothes.

"Good idea." Roger changed quickly. This new set was finer, draping more elegantly as if it was meant to be worn in front of a King. "I'll try to keep these ones cleaner."

"I'll get the first set washed." Voz'ci tied up his bundle and hoisted it. "Let's get going before my feet refuse to move."

"Right. Leave your blades and bow here. I don't want any misunderstanding."

Roger headed toward the Sombi walled village, as he stepped out of the jungle, he spread his arms and hands to show he was unarmed. Voz'ci walked with his hands away from his side.

One of the workers saw them and said something to a guard. The Sombi turned to peer at them, then checked his weapon.

That thing is loaded, don't get him angry.

The guard trotted over.

"What do you want?" He spoke heavily accented Congu. Legend said they started as one tribe, but if so, it was so long ago, they no longer could speak to each other.

"My King has sent me as a herald to speak to your King." Roger turned his hands to make the point. "I am unarmed."

"What about him?" The Sombi half pointed his weapon at Voz'ci.

"He is my Right Arm. He carries a blade as a gift for your King, but no other."

"Show me."

Roger nodded at Voz'ci who unrolled the bundle and laid out everything for the Sombi to inspect. The man glanced briefly at Bh'ob's handiwork.

"Pack this in the centre of the bundle so it cannot be reached quickly." The Sombi watched Voz'ci, then nodded and put his rifle on his shoulder. "This way, you may speak to the Commander."

"Thank you." Roger spoke in Sombi, blessing the language lessons his father had insisted on.

The Sombi raised a brow but said nothing.

They walked along the path to the fence. At the gate, their guard explained quickly, glancing at Roger. The warriors at the gate shrugged, then escorted Roger and Voz'ci, one in front and one behind. Both carried pistols on their belt. Prickles ran up and down Roger's back.

The village looked peaceful and prosperous. Sombi families walked on the road, some bargained with shop keepers. This was not something which had just sprung up. It had to have been years. Roger tried to estimate by the weathering on the buildings, but he didn't know enough.

They pulled up in front of a Kraal. The warriors exchanged brief words, then their escort led them into the building. They stopped at a door.

"You will wait here. Do not try to leave." Roger and Voz'ci walked into the small room. The door closed and a thump told Roger a bar had been dropped in place.

"Not bad." He turned in a circle, putting a finger on his lips. Voz'ci nodded. "A mat, water, a bucket with a lid. I would expect nothing less from our hosts."

Voz'ci dropped the bundle beside the mat.

"Leave that packed for now, if it will help to make them feel secure." Roger poured a little water into a cup and sipped at it. It tasted clean. He shrugged and drank a full cup.

When a couple of hours had passed with no ill effect, Roger waved Voz'ci to the water. They waited without talking. Roger expected whoever was listening would at least understand Congu, for the same reasons he spoke Sombi. Even if Voz'ci spoke Anglian or another Locasian language, using it would only raise suspicions.

A knock on the door signalled a warrior coming in with a tray of food. He glanced at the bundle and relaxed slightly. Roger thanked him. Then waved Voz'ci to the meal.

"Eat, if they meant us harm, they would have done it already."

They finished the food on the tray. Voz'ci stacked the dishes neatly, making sure all the utensils, blunt as they were, lay exposed. He put it by the door.

"You might as well get some rest." Roger nodded at the mat. "I'm too wound up to sleep yet."

Voz'ci lay down and closed his eyes.

The popular stories of the Sombi made them out to be demonic savages with no honour. Roger's father had gone to great lengths to inform his sons differently.

"They are our enemies, but they are honourable by their own rules. Those rules are different than ours, and making a mistake can kill you, but if you follow them, you'll stay alive."

The first rule was personal honour was much more important. Even a higher rank would hesitate to insult someone. Honour was measured by the authority granted the person. They did not view the hunt in the same manner as the Congu. They were deadly warriors, but pragmatic and willing to take what action they needed to win.

The second rule was the one Roger hoped to use to his benefit. Very careful knowledge of obligations and debts wound through their culture. A helpful deed by one tribe might carry obligation for generations to another. If he could hint they would hold a debt against the Congu, they would be more willing to let him speak, and deepen the debt.

No one disturbed them through the night, a tray arrived in the morning and a fresh bucket. The warriors didn't speak to them, and Roger did not talk to them other than to thank them.

They waited out another day, Roger taught Voz'ci a finger game to pass the time. The young man learned quickly and soon challenged Roger.

After a second night, a warrior knocked on the door, but instead of handing them a tray, he motioned for them to follow.

Roger and Voz'ci were walked through halls of wood, with clay packed in the joints. The construction was different than Roger was used to. He could imagine advantages, but fire would be a tremendous risk. Maybe in this damp climate it wasn't as much of a problem.

They were escorted into a large room filled with men. Warriors stood around the walls, and an older man sat on a chair lifted on a slight dais. Voz'ci stiffened beside him as he saw the Kershians. The young man may have seen Locasians on the docks, but these men didn't look like sailors. They wore uniforms and held guns which made the rifles the Sombi carried look ancient.

Their leader, a captain by his insignia, sneered at Roger.

"Another savage, as if they could stand against the Empire." He spoke in Kershian. The head Sombi frowned but didn't appear to understand the insult. Roger didn't intend to translate. The Kershians would only call him a liar.

"What say you, herald?" The man on the chair spoke good Congu.

"My King has sent me to bring greetings to your King." Roger said.

"What does Congu have to say to Sombi?"

"The Congu and Sombi are enemies, but the Sombi are known as honourable enemies. My King would talk of the changing world." Roger glanced at the frowns on the Kershians and stopped there. They would be trouble. The Empire's rules were very different from either Sombi or Congu. They only concerned themselves about the Empire's power. If they'd set their eyes on Harasah, it could only mean grief for all who dwelt here.

"I see." The man nodded. "I am ttaoku, headsman of yyatha on the Sombu.

"I am Hrona of the Hcazo." Roger didn't know why he lied about who he was, but his gut shouted at him to run, hide.

"Why should I send you to trouble my King?" ttaoku glowered at Roger.

"I would be indebted for your help." Roger kept his voice even as the Kershians muttered to each other. He couldn't hear their words and concentrate on his own.

"What is Congu debt worth?" The words came out as a sneer.

"I know not, but I humbly offer what I may."

Ttaoku rubbed his chin and stared at Roger.

"Come on, you can't be seriously thinking of letting this dirt travel to your King." The Kershian Captain stepped toward the headsman. A clatter from the walls indicated the Sombi were making their weapons ready. The Captain snarled but stepped back.

"If I do not and the King learns…" ttaoku trailed off.

"Who is going to tell him?" The Captain waved his hand at the room. "You can order any man here killed."

"I have no such authority." Ttaoku glared at the Kershian. If the expressions on the others were any indication, the Kershian was playing a very dangerous game.

"Well I do." The Captain pulled his pistol. "My Emperor trusts me."

Guns all around the room pointed at the Kershians. The Captain put up his hands and carefully returned his gun to his holster.

"When they lower their guns, kill them all, these savages need to learn who's in charge now." He muttered in Kershian to his fellows.

"Ready," Roger whispered to Voz'ci. "They are going to attack; we are going to stop them." The Captain looked over at Roger, doubt crossing his face, but the Sombi warriors slowly lowered their guns as their headsman waved at them to. The Kershians gripped their rifles. Theirs had magazines letting them shoot without reloading. They didn't raise the weapons past their hips before they started shooting. Sombi fell, but the warriors raised their own weapons.

Roger dove forward as the Captain drew his gun and aimed at ttaoku. The shot missed as Roger slammed into him. Voz'ci drove into the midst of the Kershians and disrupted their attack. The Sombi returned fire as Roger carried the Captain to the floor and wrestled for control of the pistol. The Captain slammed Roger in the face with the butt of his gun, then turned it to shoot at point blank range. Roger struck the gun with his left hand and drove his right elbow into the man's throat with all his weight behind it. The gun clattered to the floor as the man's face turned purple before he spasmed once and went still.

The room was quiet. Roger didn't want to lift his head to see the damage, but he had to.

Sombi warriors and others lay on the floor still, or moaning. Half the warriors were down. The others held their guns with white knuckled grips. The Kershians had all fallen. Only one looked like he still lived, but Roger couldn't guess for how long. Voz'ci lay in the center of them, holding his side. Roger crawled over to him.

"Sorry," Voz'ci winced and grit his teeth. "I can't go any further." He closed his eyes. "I've failed you as your Right Arm.

"Failed?" Roger picked him up and carried him to a table. "Cloths for a bandage, and something to stop the bleeding if you have it." The Sombi offered him strips torn from their own clothes. A warrior ran out and returned with a poultice. He helped Roger tie the bandage.

"We will care for him as one of our own."

Roger took stock of his body, a burn across his back let him know how close he had come to joining Voz'ci. Blood dripped from his forehead. So much for keeping this set of white clothes clean. A shout of rage erupted from him, and the Sombi joined him with ululating war cries.

"You understand the foreigners." Ttaoku's arm oozed blood from a bullet wound.

"I do." Roger admitted.

"You are more than Hrona of Hcazo."

"I am."

"The King must know of this treachery."

"If I may." Roger saluted the headsman. "We must not seem like we are in a rush or carry important news." He waved at the carnage. "The Kershians see your King as little different than you. They are like ants. Countless in number and hard to kill the whole nest."

"Ants." Ttaoku nodded. "Ddokna, escort the Herald to our King. You will report to any who ask that we have trouble with ants. Give the ants no hint we know their nature. Hrona, these men are interested in rocks on the Congu side of the river. I suspect they have been talking to Mtuaka and offering him the same they offered us. Power to do as we will."

"Cotus flowers." Roger closed his eyes. "They taste sweet, but they are addictive and will kill you in the end."

"I know them." Ttaoku grimaced. "Warriors will travel the old ways to let other tribes know of this treachery. I cannot promise they will listen."

Roger saluted once more.

"I need to borrow some clothing. A herald is dangerous to the Kershians. If I travel as a prisoner taken to the King to report…"

"As you will. Ddokna will see you have what you need. Until your task is closed, he will be your Right Arm."

A Sombi warrior stepped forward and saluted in their style, fist against forehead instead of heart.

"Take care of my man." Roger said.

"We will."

"Come," ddokna said to Roger. "I will get you clothing, then we cross the river tonight. The train leaves in the morning. We must be on it."

"Lead on." Roger gave one last look and salute to Voz'ci then left the room.

***

Tashi brought in new clothes for llathia to wear.

"The forester wanted you to be properly dressed for the jungle."

"May as well, it isn't like there is anyone to impress." Llathia put the tunic and skirt on. Tashi looked ready to complain, but shrugged instead.

"Let's go before there is too much traffic in the hallways."

They wove through the Staal.

"Is there a reason the hallways are so confusing?" llathia asked as they rounded yet another corner.

"Yes." Tashi stopped short. "Whatever you do, don't speak until I give you the word."

Llathia looked down the hall to see a tall man, striding toward them a leer fixed on his face.

"What have we here?" He stood blocking the hall to peer down at Tashi and Ilathia. "I haven't seen either of you before. Come with me."

"We are expected somewhere. The Prince would be most displeased if we are late."

"Bah, the Princes…" A growl from behind Ilathia made the man look up as if he'd just noticed Chiza. "You going to challenge a guest of your King in his own halls?"

"Guest rights do not extend to harassing the King's servants." Thasi stepped in front of Ilathia

"A servant is going to tell me what I can and can't do?" the man's face grew dark and his hand dropped to his waist.

"Perhaps, we should go to my father and clarify the matter." Tzoca strolled around a corner. "I believe he is speaking with Mtuaka in his chamber." He glared at Ilathia. "You are late. Go."

Tashi took Ilathia's hand and practically ran down the corner leaving Tzoca facing the man.

"Will he be all right?" Ilathia gasped out as they ran.

"Bura will be close at hand. The Second Prince prefers subtlety over threat."

Llathia chanced a glance back at Chiza, who jogged easily, but with a face set in stone.

The foresters were just gathering when Tashi and Ilathia burst into their midst. They saw Chiza and kept whatever questions they had to themselves.

A short time later, the Second Prince strolled in. The men stood at attention and saluted.

"A slight change of plans." He drawled the words, but Ilathia picked up the rage beneath them. "You were going to go out, pick a few trees, then return immediately. I have decided it would be better for the engine-smith to be present for the harvesting of the trees to give her opinion on which we should take. Since this will mean a longer stay, her maid will accompany her. The Third Prince's Right Arm has been assigned to the engine-smith and I will not argue with his reasons. Be assured he will not be in your way. If you need anything beyond what you've packed, let my storesmaster know and he will send it to you." The prince nodded once, then spun and left, not even glancing in Ilathia's direction.

He is angry at me.

The man who had talked to her mother the day before stepped forward.

"What will you need?"

"Ilathia will need at least one more set of clothes and a larger tent. I will need what is required to serve her properly." Tashi spoke up. Llathia half expected the storesmaster to take offence at her tone, but he only nodded at her. The men listed other things ranging from food to equipment. The man didn't take any notes, but Ilathia felt sure he could have repeated their list exactly.

"Please." Ilathia lifted her hand slightly. "Carry my greetings to my mother."

The storesmaster saluted her, then when there were no more requests, he left. The men spoke quietly while sneaking looks at Ilathia.

"Now they are wondering who you are that the Prince's storesmaster salutes you. He doesn't salute anyone but royalty." Tashi whispered.

"Oh." Llathia twisted her fingers. She had to prove her worth, and now everyone would be nervous around her.

"They would anyway." Tashi flashed a grin at Ilathia. "No normal person has a Right Arm following them, certainly not Chiza.

They packed up what they had into a cart, then set the oxen moving. The animals moved at a comfortable walking pace even for Ilathia and Tashi.

"Engine-smith." A man separated himself from the group. "If you would like, I can identify the trees we pass."

"That would be nice," Ilathia said, "I can identify the lumber from the trees, but have little idea what the tree looks like."

The morning passed with him pointing out trees and discussing with Ilathia the uses of the lumber.

"Where did you learn the wood?" Xinke asked. Llathia had finally convinced him to give his name.

"My father had a lumber yard. He ran the saws with a steam engine he'd built himself." She caught a sob back, Xinke drifted back to the others.

"They will have heard the stories, mistress. Grief is allowed." Tashi's face appeared drawn and older than it should be, then her smile returned.

Llathia wondered at the annual trip to visit family. Tashi had never said they were living.

They stopped for lunch and one of the other foresters, who had known her father somewhat, came over to extend his condolences.

After lunch, the young woman were left to walk alone. Llathia missed the dialogue with the forester but didn't know how to bridge the gap.

"It is better if there is a little distance." Tashi said, with her uncanny ability to know what llathia was thinking. "You are the engine-smith, you may want discussion, but not argument. Given a chance they will all inform you of what is best."

Late in the afternoon they arrived at a grove of bottle trees. The men unhitched the oxen and worked at setting camp. Llathia pulled out the memory of her father's stories about his engine.

"Chiza, I could use a stick. Not too heavy, but solid. A knot on the end would be useful." Llathia stayed close to Tashi, though the girl expressed horror at the idea that llathia would help.

A few minutes later Chiza presented llathia with a stick which fit her standards perfectly.

"I should say I'm surprized." Llathia hefted the stick. "But I'm not in the slightest. I wonder if you are actually some magical being."

Chiza's mouth twitched.

"Come, I want to bang on some trees. Try to look like you believe I know what I'm doing."

His mouth twitched again.

Llathia sauntered over to the first tree and whacked it with her stick, she shook her head. "Not hollow enough, if at all." One after the other she attacked the trees in the grove. A couple of them she circled around hitting them on each side. Occasionally she would catch a forester peering at her.

"Mark this one." She pointed at a tree she'd just circled a second time. "We'll have some work to even it out, but it is a good start." By the time Tashi came to fetch her for supper, llathia had marked two trees.

"Your father taught you well." Xinke said to her after they'd finished eating and Tashi had explained she was the engine-smith's maid, not theirs. "You picked the two I would have probably chosen based on the description we were given." He pointed his chin at the others who were still grumbling about doing dishes. "They will argue with you. Stick to your choices."

He strolled over to the pile of dishes and began washing them, humming slightly. The others saw and threw their hands in the air.

Llathia had the feeling the conversation around the fire would have been much livelier without her presence. She announced that she was retiring to her tent long before she wanted to.

Tashi had laid out the tent to feel as close to llathia's room in the Staal as possible.

"You're amazing." Llathia sat on the stool in one corner.

"Anything for my princess." Tashi saluted and grinned.

"Tell me more about that man we met this morning."

"Oh him." Tashi made a face like she'd bitten into a rotten fruit. "Ntoox, he's the heir to Mtuaka, and he's as brutish as they come. He's never stayed in the Staal without leaving some servant expecting a child. I'm told he doesn't take no for an answer. My Prince won't have him in the Kraal. None of the Princes like him, but for some reason, the man has a special hate for the Third Prince. Mtuaka is as bad, but he forces people to marry their daughters to him, the younger the better. He says it's because he's trying for an heir. The heir to the Ynoke tribe refused to let the man marry his young sister. She couldn't have been more than ten or eleven years at the time. His father had agreed and the King all but ordered him to produce the girl, but the heir refused, and the King banished him. Mtuaka wanted his head, but as heir he hadn't sworn directly to the King yet. Mtuaka is still searching for the girl from what I heard, but he won't find her."

"You sound very certain." Llathia stretched until her back popped.

"I'm Ynoke." Tashi glared at the door as if Ntoox might walk in. "What we hide, stays hidden."

"Good for you."

"Going back to Ntoox, if he corners you, make as much noise as you can. You are a guest of the King, not a servant. Technically, you are working on behalf of the Third Prince, so only he can give permission for someone to take you, and lions are more likely to dance than he will let Ntoox have anything he wants. Servants are hard to make a fuss about, though I'm told the King is enraged whenever it happens. He could challenge Ntoox, and make no mistake. the King may look old and relaxed, but there is no warrior who can hope to touch him."

"I will be spending most of my time working on the engine, and the rest covered in grease. I will hardly be attractive."

"I hope that's enough." Tashi frowned. "I don't know what would happen if Chiza attacked the beast. It would be a nightmare."

***

"We will cut the trees I marked." Llathia swung her stick gently. "None of the others are suitable. If there is another grove close, I can go check on them. If not, I'll make do with two, but it means no mistakes."

"We should cut one or two of the others." A forester standing back from the others crossed his arms and glared at her truculently.

"Why waste the trees? They aren't suitable."

"And how do you know that, missy? I heard you talking on the road, you don't know trees any better than that maid of yours."

Fire exploded in Ilathia's gut. She stalked over to the man. Holding her stick tight in one hand.

"You cut the trees I marked, because I marked them. You will cut them the way I tell you because I tell you. Are you going to build the king an engine out of those trees?" She swept the stick to point it at him. "Either you do what you're told, or you start walking." She pointed back down the road.

"And why would I do that? You going to make with that stick of yours. You just try." He puffed out his chest and stepped up close to her.

The flames which fueled her word flared up bright. Before she thought of it, the stick jammed into the man's gut. When he grunted and bent over, she brought the ball on the end of the stick down on his head. He dropped to the ground like a stone and didn't move.

"Chiza, when he wakes up, make sure he starts walking back to the Staal. If he's smart, he'll keep walking to somewhere they won't mind the noise he makes." She spun and pointed to the first of the marked trees. "Any others want to discuss my qualifications?" When the whole group shook their heads in unison, llathia came close to giggling. "Let's get started."

The men began the work glancing over at llathia constantly to make sure they were doing the right thing, but as the day passed, she kept her orders polite and consistent. They relaxed and chatted as they climbed to find the top of the hollow, then cut the tree off well above the empty space. The lower cut was much more difficult as the space extended below the ground. Llathia feared she'd made a mistake, but the men were able to dig deep enough to cut below the hollow. The sun was low in the sky by the time they'd finished.

"Good work." Llathia called them over. "We will cut the other tree tomorrow. Relax for the evening and rest."

"Pardon, engine-smith." The man who'd known her father raised his hand. "How are we going to get the thing back to the Staal? It's too big to fit in a wagon."

Llathia looked at the massive section of trunk. It was half again as big as her father's. *How did father move logs?* The image of a line of logs letting the larger one roll easily into the blade came to her. *Thanks, Father.*

"We will cut smaller rounds and roll it along. The oxen should be able to handle it."

A few of the men shook their heads and laughed.

"Sorry, engine-smith. We should have thought of that ourselves. Just never done it with a trunk that big."

"Remember it is hollow, so it will be lighter than it looks."

Xinke came over when the others went to revive the fire and start on supper.

"You did good, mistress. You was fair, and didn't punish him until he asked for it. All the men here will work themselves to the bone for you." There was a hint of warning in his tone. Llathia turned it over in her mind.

"If you think they are working too hard, tell me. I don't want any injuries."

Xinke sighed, then saluted her before rejoining the other foresters.

Llathia escaped to the tent where she tossed the club into a corner.

"I don't know what came over me." She dropped on the stool and put her head in her hands.

"The Sombi are a warrior people as much as the Congu." Tashi came to stand behind llathia and massaged her shoulders. "You could have had Chiza do it. He was on his toes ready to move. I think you surprised him as much as anyone else. What you did was better. They won't be looking to see if Chiza is there to back you up. You also switched from warrior princess to reasonable engine-smith and showed you won't abuse them."

"I didn't even plan it." Llathia leaned into Tashi's hands. "He challenged me, then bam, he was lying on the ground. I didn't even worry I'd killed him."

"He woke up and took off down the road like a lion was chasing him." Tashi paused her hands and leaned forward to speak with her lips almost touching llathia's ears. "You need to understand; you used the privileges of a noble. They accept it because you have me and Chiza, but take great care if the situation comes up again."

Llathia nodded and Tashi's fingers started up again.

They cut the other tree and the men said they could get the trunks back to the Staal without her. It would take a week to cover the distance they'd walked in a day. So llathia, and Tashi set off with Chiza back to Lusundi. She carried the stick on her shoulder.

Ok, they've accepted me as the engine-smith. Now I'd better produce the engine.

Chapter 7 Spooked Game

Roger followed ddokna to the river. It had been hidden on the other side of the village. The Sombu might have been an ocean but for a faint line which hinted at a far shore.

"Good thing the water is still high. The river-horses won't bother us."

"Why would they bother us?" Roger gazed at the water, entranced.

"They don't like boats."

"Voz'ci, my Right Arm, hunted a river-horse on his first hunt. I never got to hear the story."

"He is a worthy warrior, no matter what side of the river he was born." Ddokna humphed. "Most of us in this area are mixed from centuries of raiding."

"The guns have changed that." Roger forced his hand away from the poultice on his back. "Now there is death instead of life. Voz'ci introduced me to a girl, maybe his age, maybe younger. She looked pure Sombi. Her mother is the reason I'm here."

"What's her mother's name?"

"nnontui, she was married to a Congu who built a steam engine from wood."

"I don't like to stand near the steam engines the foreigners brought, and they is all steel, more than Sombi could mine in a year. I can't imagine a wood one."

"Neither could I until I saw it. She is going to build another one."

"The mother?" ddokna turned to stare at Roger.

"The daughter."

"We have a legend in our tribe." Ddokna walked along planks set in the mud. "If a crocodile charges, run. Even the rifles won't stop them." He pointed out into the mud, things Roger had taken for logs until one of them moved.

"You mentioned a legend?"

"My tribe has lived here for centuries. The other tribes sneer at us because of our Congu blood. The old people talk about a child who will be born ebony black with the bones of a queen. She will save us from a terrible enemy."

"That sounds like an awful burden to put on a young girl." They stepped from the planks to a dock which stretched far out into the river.

"That's why it is also seen as bad luck to look too Sombi."

Roger laughed.

The boat was a large flat thing, smoke came from its stack. Ddokna tossed the bundle of Roger's things onto the deck.

"The foreigners were jealous of their machines and wouldn't let any of us work them. But I watched." Ddokna shovelled coal into the firebox. Roger picked up a piece and looked at it.

"Did they bring this in?"

"No, we mine it to the north." Ddokna tapped on the gauge and twisted a couple of valves.

"You mine it, and they use it."

"It came so slowly we didn't notice. A foreigner needing a guide to find rocks. Who needs rocks?" More levers and the engine began chugging. Ddokna ran up and down the dock untying the boat before jumping back on and moving another lever. They started moving backwards away from the dock. He steered them in a broad circle then reversed the position of the last lever, the boat glided forward sending ripples up and down the water. A river-horse roared as it to let them know this was their river. "They wanted to build a railway, to open up the interior they said. Make travel from Biafa to the Sombu faster. I don't remember it ever being too slow, but they are like that with their machines. All about power and speed."

"Like a lion searching for bigger teeth." Roger leaned against the doorway and watched ddokna work.

"Exactly." Ddokna pointed upriver and Roger spotted the immense head of a river-horse. Birds flew around them. Occasionally one would land on the boat to rest.

I don't understand why we are enemies.

"Now the foreigners have shown their teeth. They crawl like ants through Biafa and the King is never alone without one whispering in his ear. I fear they will not leave if we ask them."

"It depends on how you do the asking." Roger said, and ddokna grinned ferociously.

"Understanding is possible between old enemies." Ddokna said. "But I cannot understand the foreigners."

"They are insatiable." Roger shrugged. "Whatever they have they want more. Their poor live like royalty, their royalty…that's beyond imagining, yet they think they don't have enough."

"You know a lot about these foreigners."

"It is why the King made me his herald."

Ddokna maneuvered the boat next to the dock on the Sombi side of the river. He reversed the levers and valves then jumped onto the dock. Roger helped

106

him tie up the boat, then picked up his bundle and settled it on his back.

At the end of the dock, ddokna pointed to a large mound not far from the path the boards followed. The distance looked shorter on this side.

"He will charge when we get close. Run like the wind and you'll learn if you can outrun a crocodile."

"I don't need to outrun the crocodile." Roger grinned. "I just need to be faster than you." He jumped onto the boards and loped along them until he was at the closest to the huge reptile.

"Hey, lizard wake up."

The beast shifted from dead still to a full-out run in a second. Roger sprinted along the planks laughing while ddokna cursed behind him.

"You are crazy." Ddokna slapped him on the back. "For a Congu, you're all right."

He led Roger along a path which opened out to a railway station built in the middle of the jungle. It looked like the Kershian stations he'd seen as he travelled Locasia between terms of university.

"Come on, we need to talk to the station master."

"He talks Sombi like a monkey."

"Maybe we can teach the monkey some new tricks."

"I can run the river boat because I've seen how it's done. They've never let any Sombi near their engine."

"I'll keep that in mind."

They climbed the stairs onto the station. For the first time since meeting Cal, he missed his Anglian clothes. Standing on a platform with the engine hissing, made him feel uncomfortable in his Congu attire. Roger squashed the feeling as ddokna walked over to the ticket window.

"I have a prisoner to take to Biafa." He spoke slowly and clearly.

"What?" the ticketmaster shouted in Kershian. "Speak properly. Only Kershian on this railway." The others standing near laughed at him.

"Let me try." Roger pulled ddokna back from the window. He sauntered up to the window and leaned heavily on it. "Listen, tinpot." Roger spoke in a Mzorat accent. "If you blow my mission getting your jollies, I will see to it the Emperor himself learns your name." The stationmaster paled and backed up as far as he could go. "Well hurry up, and say nothing to anyone, or I'll come back and gut you myself." The man passed over Roger two tickets, his hands shaking. Once Roger had them, the man slammed the shutters closed and the thump of a bar dropping sounded from the other side.

"Let's get on the train." Roger waved the tickets and picked up his bundle. They climbed onto the car ddokna said was for the Sombi. Hard benches, no softness anywhere. He thought the Sombi would scoff at too much softness. They might not realize the insult. Then he saw the tight anger on ddokna's face.

"What did you say to the stationmaster?" ddokna asked.

"Told him I was a Kershian spy." Roger grinned

"Are you?"

"I understand them too well to work for them."

They sat in a seat furthest from the Kershian carriage, Roger's bundle at his feet. After another half hour, the Kershians climbed onto their carriage between them and the engine. Roger watched as they carried their guns with them. The stationmaster was the only Kershian he'd seen without a gun at hand.

The train jerked a couple of times then slowly picked up speed until the jungle passed in a blur. The car grew warm and stuffy. At least the Kershians had to suffer the same heat. The jungle on either side of them vanished and the train rocketed across a broad plain.

The door at the other end of the car opened and three Kershians strutted into the car. The lead man wore a Colonel's uniform.

"I don't know who you are." He spoke to Roger sneering down at arm's length from him, ignoring ddokna. "But no one informed me of any intelligence work in this area. You savages need to keep your place." He turned to go. "Shoot them both."

Roger lunged out of his seat, wrapped an arm around the Colonel's throat and pulled the man's pistol from his belt. The two soldiers hesitated when faced with shooting their own officer. Roger shot them both. He slugged the Colonel with the butt of the man's own gun.

"Grab their guns. Work the bolt this way." He demonstrated. "Keep pulling the trigger, you don't need to reload." Roger dropped the Colonel and dove for one gun as ddokna picked up the other. Two Kershians came through the door to investigate the gun shots. Roger dropped one, ddokna the other. The rest of them tried a rush through the door and took heavy casualties for their efforts. Roger took magazines from the two he'd shot and reloaded his gun and passed it to ddokna, then loaded his.

"If they're smart, they'll shoot through the walls." Roger considered whether it would be worth trying take the ammunition from the bodies at the other end of the car. Ddokna interrupted his thoughts by spraying the end wall with his bullets. Roger shrugged and passed him the loaded weapon. The Sombi emptied it too.

"We need to get off the train." Roger looked around for what he had seen in every Kershian carriage he'd ever ridden on. *There*.

"Throw the bundle out, then get ready to toss the Colonel and jump yourself." He sprinted for the brake cable and heaved on it with all his strength. The car slowed suddenly as the wheels screeched on the track. Gunfire from the other car pockmarked the ceiling.

"Go, hurry, it won't slow long." Roger followed ddokna who threw the Colonel's body out, then hesitated. Roger pushed him, then leaped away from the train. It shrank into the distance. Roger didn't hear anything to suggest they were going to slow and come after them. The train vanished in the distance.

He found ddokna by the sound of his laughter.

"Crazy Congu." The man stood and dusted himself off. "Just like jumping off a charging elephant."

"You've done that?" Roger raised his brow.

"No, never could get on." Ddokna laughed harder. The Colonel groaned.

"He said he knew everything about the operations in this area." Roger roped the man's arms together with his necktie. A quick search revealed matches, a pipe, ammunition for the pistol which lay on the floor of the train. A knife almost escaped Roger's notice it blended into the boot so well.

"We need to find some Sombi. I have to warn my people that we just started a war with the foreigners."

"We will warn them, but we didn't start the war. It's been going on for years. Now you have the chance to fight back."

Ddokna stared at him with his mouth open. "Are you sure you're not a Kershian spy?"

"Of course I'm a spy, but not for them." Roger headed down the track. "I need to find my bundle, then we'll find your people."

A tiny woman stepped out of the grass holding a long tube. "What's this about a war?"

***

llathia inspected the field she'd been given to build the engine.

"We hold games up here occasionally, but there aren't many people around to ask questions." The First Prince put his hands on his hips. "You will need some shelter, or you'll die of the heat."

"I need rope, as heavy as you can find, and as much. Pitch too. A saw, more wood. Logs straight and close to the same size as the tubes. Oh, and cloth, and grease. We'll need endless amounts of grease. Stones we can put between the fire and the tank." Llathia pulled out the drawing she'd made and tried to think if she'd missed anything, then shook her head. "I could stand here from dawn to dusk listing things I need. Let's start with the stones. Dig a pit here, then put a stone slab across it. It will keep the tree from catching fire."

"You don't want the tree burning?" The prince furrowed his brow.

"No, trust me. If you see the tank burning, run as fast as you can away from the thing."

"I will arrange for the stone." The First Prince left almost like he imagined the bottle tree burning.

"Can I really do this?" llathia held her head in her hands and crouched on the ground.

"Of course you can, llathia." Chiza spoke behind her. "Trust your father's knowledge in you."

"What if I fail?" She looked up at him through her fingers.

"Everyone fails." Chiza reached down and hauled her to her feet. "Roger failed one exam three times, but each time he did better, until he passed. Failure is a goad for learning."

"Thanks." Llathia leaned her head against Chiza's chest. She took a deep breath and straightened. "You didn't call me a fool."

"Next time." Chiza said.

"I want to talk to Bh'ob about the tubes. If we can't make them of metal, I'll have to use more hollow trees." She led the way down the hill. They arrived at the Staal to have the warriors at the gate inform them they, and all llathia's stuff had been moved up to the First Prince's Kraal.

The move brought her closer to her work, but his baths weren't as nice as the ones at the Staal. She could live with that.

***

The foresters arrived with the tree. Llathia had the pit set up the way she wanted; its stone walls held flat slabs. The whole thing was level. The builder complained the King's floor wasn't that level. Llathia told him she wasn't building a steam engine on the King's floor.

A huge coil of rope lay to one side. A cauldron rested over another fire pit.

"Right. We'll work on the smaller one first. It will be easier." They set it on the rocks, tilted it over and shaved at the bottom until it stood straight enough for her.

"Now we need holes cut here." She thumped the tank with her club. "This size." She drew a circle on the trunk. "On the other side, here." Another thump. "Smaller." She scratched another circle.

Once the holes were cut and Ilathia was satisfied they were as perfect as they could manage, she crawled through the larger hole and inspected the inside of the tree. She spent a day smoothing the inside, then putting the shavings in baskets to remove them from the space. When they covered the holes, she saw no light.

"Looks good." She climbed out and arranged her clothes properly. "Now we melt the pitch and coat the trunk with it, then wrap the rope around it as tight as we can. Two layers. While you get started on the bottom, I'll get the steam pipe and the water feed in place."

Bh'ob and his smiths had worked miracles. One of them had talked to an Anglian who mentioned rolled steel. They'd experimented until they could make sheets large enough to bend and weld into pipes. The water pipe was first. She'd given them a tracing of the hole and the pipe they'd made was a marvel. She almost forgot to put in the valve. A piece of steel which fit exactly in the pipe, then mounted to let water in, but not allow steam to escape. With that and wooden supports they fit the pipe. Llathia climbed in with a file, a bucket of pitch and the biggest hammer she could swing.

The file cut into the steel almost to the wood of the tree. She stuck her head out the hole and shouted instructions for someone to file the large pipe a hand's length from the end fitting in the tree.

The pitch packed in around the pipe as deep as she could force it. They'd already done the outside. Then she wielded the hammer to bend the steel to lay flat against the wood. More pitch, more hammering until she was satisfied.

"OK, let's get the big one in place." Llathia shouted.

"How will you get out?" Xinke's voice came back.

"Through the pipe. I made it big enough. *I hope.*

The bigger pipe started off easier. She didn't need to file, but there was more pitch to pack. The men pushed buckets with sticks until she could reach them. Then she hammered. The steel of this pipe was thicker and didn't want to bend. But llathia was remorseless and forced the metal to her will. By the time she had finished, barely any light gleamed through the end of the pipe. She tossed the bucket down the pipe, then with aching arms heaved the hammer along it too.

When she crawled into the pipe, she got halfway before it narrowed. She fit, but neither her fingers nor toes could get enough purchase to move her.

"Pass me the stick." She shouted. "I need you to pull me out."

The stick came slowly until she grabbed it and held on until her hands ached.

"Pull slowly, go."

The metal of the pipe scraped at her, picked at her clothes, then her skin. She shrank herself as small as she could until hands took hers and lifted her out. The air stung on her skin. Llathia looked down and saw there was little left of her clothes but rags. One of the men wrapped her in his own tunic, then two others made a seat with their hands and carried her like a queen down to the Kraal.

***

A group worked on the pistons to fit in the cylinders the smiths made. Four of them.

"Right." Llathia circle the tank one last time. "Put the water in, then close the valve. Light the fire and we'll heat the tank for a pressure test."

They'd found a skinny woman to slide in the greased pipe to set the pressure control valve. Now it was time to find out if their work had paid off.

All day they fed the fire and watched where the tank rested on the stone for signs of scorching. The heat would boil the water in the tank, but the temperature of the water would stay below what was needed to light the wood aflame. That was the theory, and her father had made it work.

Hints of steam came from the valve on the water pipe. She had them rope the lever to hold it closed. The steam stopped.

The valve in the steam pipe held well, and the men congratulated the woman who'd placed it. They watched and waited for the pressure valve she'd watched her father fix a hundred time to move. It trembled but refused to move. Llathia walked close to tap it with her stick.

The tank was hissing. She prowled around the tank until she found the source. It came out from between the ropes about shoulder height.

"Shut it down." Llathia shouted. "It's not going to work." She wanted to smash the trunk with her stick, break it into pieces for daring to fail.

"What now?" one of the men asked.

"Tomorrow we take this one apart then start on the other."

Chapter 8 A New Hunt

Roger and ddokna were escorted to a village hidden on the plain. Hiloto moved her warriors with tiny flicks of her fingers. One of them carried Roger's bundle. She stopped the group with an upraised hand, then after the unseen danger had passed, they continued with a finger flipped forward.

She could have walked beneath Roger's outstretched arm without ducking. Ddokna looked around nervously. Roger put his hand on the man's arm and nodded when he turned his face. He didn't relax but he did look less likely to run at a moment's notice.

They had almost entered the village before Roger saw it. Hiloto pointed to a spot beside the fire burning in a deep pit.

"You may talk, quietly." Hiloto smiled at them. "Thank you for your silence on the stalk."

Other men and women came with gourds with water for Hiloto and her group. A man handed one to Roger and ddokna.

"Because of where we get our water, you may find it disconcerting." He smiled at Roger.

"He means if you drink it you will hallucinate." Ddokna made a sour face at the gourd, then shrugged and drank it down. Roger followed suit.

The man crouched beside Roger.

"If you talk about what you see, I can help you to know what is real and what is illusion."

Ddokna shuffled over to where a woman crouched.

Roger couldn't get a read on anyone's ages. He'd see a girl, only to realize when she got close that her face was painted with wrinkles, a man would walk through the clearing only to break into a game of tag with other children. Hiloto crouched in front of him, and her face wavered between a smooth faced girl and a wrinkled crone.

Words poured out of him describing what he saw, then giants loomed over the village, piercing men, women and children with spears, before devouring them. A lion with dagger like teeth attacked the giants.

When Roger returned his gaze to the village the people were going about their work as if nothing had happened.

A wall of flamed approach with the speed of a charging elephant. The people didn't run, but lay in holes and covered themselves with animal skins. The fire passed and they climbed out and continued their lives.

Grinding noises came from one side. The people looked toward them, puzzlement clear on their faces, then huge metal machines appeared, spewing smoke and sparks. Fire spread in all directions. The machines rolled over the village leaving mangle corpses behind. With a flicker, everything returned to normal.

The man at his side grinned and wandered away.

"You have been blessed with visions of past and future." Hiloto spoke from beside him. Her face weathered, no longer shifting from child to crone.

"You were a cute child." Roger said, then winced.

"Part of the effect is to speak one's thoughts. We hold no malice toward thought. Only action matters."

"Wise." He stared into the flames. "Your people have suffered through the years."

"We have also flourished. A generation ago, a wise woman walked out of the plain, accompanied by her son. They forged a peace with the tribes of the jungle." She glanced over at ddokna. "We are learning trust."

"The machines..."

"It seems you were shown a future." Hiloto shrugged. "There are many, we don't let them dictate our actions in the present."

"But you are in danger." Roger put his hands to his head. "The foreigners—a"

"The ones with the trains which throw sparks to light fires. It is why we watch. Too many fires are as bad as not enough."

"They are the kind of people to build machines to crush those in their way."

"I understand this, I've called for a meet with other tribes in the grassland. They will arrive soon. We will talk then of monsters and machines."

***

The others walked out of the grass to be welcomed by Hiloto's village. Ddokna's jaw dropped at how many gathered.

"The people outside the plain have come to speak to us of danger." Hiloto started talking with no introduction. "As grandmother fashioned a peace with the jungle tribes, we must decide whether peace is possible with the train people."

"We had to move our village. The train people shot at us with weapons that gave horrible wounds from a far distance. They laughed as they passed as if murder was a sport."

"Where the plain meets the river, the train people have burned away the grass, then ground the soil. They keep herds of slow, stupid cattle where our village once stood."

The list went on, Roger put his hand on ddokna's shoulder once, when the man looked ready to speak. When the silence extended past eight breaths, he tapped his companion's shoulder and nodded.

"The train people came from far away. They offered marvels in exchange for a place to land their ships. Then they wanted more, and more." Ddokna sighed and looked down. "We were fools. One of their leaders tried to murder our headsman for disagreeing with them. This one's friend lies injured from fighting them. Then they tried to kill us on the train, and we escaped."

"We brought the man you threw off the train." Hiloto nodded. "Let's ask him about their plans."

Three men carried the Colonel out, tied now with grass ropes. His face was red with anger and he shouted incoherently.

"He has been given water. Let us listen to his heart." The assembly tilted their heads. Roger started translating, leaving out the more pungent insults.

We will hunt you down and crush you. Only the Empire will rule. Savages, runts, worthless except as slaves..."

There was a lot more, but Roger tired of mouthing evil and fell silent.

Then the Colonel lost his anger and began detailing plans for conquering not only Sombi, but the entire continent, destroying any who got in their way.

"Soon we will kill the King. He has far too much pride. Put his daughter on the throne. A girl will be biddable, and we will own the place. Then our allies will strike to the south."

"How soon?" Roger asked. The Colonel looked at him and screamed until he frothed at the mouth and went into convulsions. When they passed, he lay lifeless on the ground.

"Is peace desirable?" Hiloto asked quietly as if the dead man hadn't just been ranting about destroying their world.

"They lack wisdom for peace." One replied, and the others nodded.

"The people of the grass have not gone to war in generations beyond number. Do we go to war?" An old man had tears running down his cheeks as he spoke.

"This one," Hiloto pointed at Roger, "said we are already at war. I believe he is wise."

"Let me say what I am going to say, then you will decide for yourselves." Roger took a long breath and held it until his heart slowed and he had washed all anger from himself. "I know this tribe, they come from far away. Most are not bad people, but their leaders are greedy. The ones who enjoy destruction are sent here. They don't see you as people, any more than they see cattle as people. It is what they have been taught, what they must believe to accomplish their King's orders.

"You cannot fight them head on. You've heard about their guns, and they have worse than that. You will need to be ghosts, play on their fear, for they all live in fear. Send messengers to the jungle people. The foreigners will send an army to destroy them for the dead on the train. I am sorry we brought this on you."

Roger looked at ddokna.

"Let the train pass, then drop the largest tree you can across the tracks, so they are trapped. Take your people into the jungle, or across the river. Then use all your knowledge of the hunt to carve away at the foreigners. Like ants, they will wander in confusion when their leaders are lost. Look for men with these images on their clothes." Roger pointed at the colonel's jacket. "Target them. If any surrender, show mercy. We live in the same world. Peace is not possible now, but it doesn't mean it never will be."

The people of the grass sat in silence while the sun moved overhead. Then they collectively sighed and stood, one by one they bowed to Hiloto, then to Roger before disappearing into the grass.

"I'd better go too." Ddokna stood and clapped Roger on the shoulder. "In the Biafa, our headsman has a cousin. He's a butcher named zzilfa. Trust him." He nodded to Hiloto then walked into the grass.

"I had better do my part." Roger stretched and stood up.

"Stay the night, then we will guide you to where the grass meets the river."

Hiloto led Roger through the endless grass. He began to hear differences in how the wind rustled it. When she stopped him, the whisper of a large animal moving tickled his ears. After two days of walking they arrived at the edge of the plain. As they had been told, the area had been ravaged, and now cattle roamed finding what food they could in the devastation.

"The herders look as fat and contented as the cattle." Hiloto shook her head. "I fear you cannot trust them. There will be canoes on the shore, take one and let the river carry you."

"Thank you." Roger saluted her. "May I have one of the gourds of water?"

Hiloto handed him the sling with the gourds, three still filled with water. "I will find what I need on the way home." She cocked her head and studied him. "You have walked strange paths, and stranger yet await you. You will shake the world."

She vanished with no word of farewell. Roger squatted in the shade of the grass and waited for nightfall.

***

Ilathia stared at the new tank, at least twice the size of her father's, willing it to hold pressure. She'd worry about high pressure later, for now, all she wanted was not to hear the hiss of escaping steam.

One of the foresters had come up with a glue to seal the inside of the tank. He hoped it would take the heat, but assured her it was waterproof. They'd worked for four days, llathia and Jintu taking turns inside the tank. She was the smallest adult she'd ever met. She claimed to have a grass person in his ancestry. She had no idea what she was talking about, but the others rolled their eyes.

The tank's shadow crept across the ground. The only way they'd know if there was pressure was by releasing and shutting the valve to the steam pipe.

"How is the tank holding up?" Bh'ob came up to llathia.

"It hasn't blown up or sprung a leak. Yet."

"Happy to hear that." He didn't sidle back when she mentioned explosions. "You wanted to talk to me about something?"

"I need a valve which will release the pressure if it gets beyond a certain point – to stop the tank from blowing." She didn't take her eyes from the tank.

"Hmm." Bh'ob scratched his head. "One of the smiths claims to have a steel which springs back into shape when bent. Perhaps a valve made of that? We'd have to balance the thickness of the steel carefully or it would open too soon or too late."

"How do we figure out what pressure is too much without blowing the tank?" llathia shuddered at the idea of going to cut more trees and starting over from scratch.

"If we want to balance the strength of the steel against the strength of the wood." Bh'ob pointed to the discarded tank. "Have a contest between steel and wood. We find out how thick a piece will crack the wood, then make it thinner."

"Half." Llathia said. "We make it half as thick, even then we're guessing, but I'd rather lose steam early than blow the tank."

"I'll see what I can rig up for you. Tomorrow?"

"Tomorrow would be a miracle." Llathia shook her head. "If the tank holds pressure, we will need to attach the cylinders and pistons, make the arms to turn the shaft. Then we will be ready for a running pressure test. That's when I need the valve."

"I'll get to work, llathia."

Fifteen minutes after he left, the steam hissed out the steam tube when the valve opened.

"It holds pressure." Llathia shouted, and the women and men around her cheered. "Rake the fire out and leave the valve open. Show me what you have done with the cylinders and piston."

When the sun dropped below the horizon, llathia sent her workers home down the hill. She patted the tank.

"Thank you." Her eyes leaked tears and llathia scrubbed at them with the back of her hand.

"I thought you were joking about the grease." Tzoca said. He caught her as her feet tangled almost sending her to the ground.

"Now, you're covered with it too." Llathia restrained the urge to try to wipe it off him.

"I heard the celebration and thought I'd come up to congratulate you."

"It's only the first step." Llathia turned and leaned against the still warm tank. Tzoca stood close to her, part of her wanted to push him back, another to pull him closer. She settled on doing nothing.

"But it is the first step." Tzoca brushed a spot of grease from her forehead. "There are stories of the engine-smith going through the city. One is that she put a man twice her size on the ground without blinking."

"He wasn't twice my size..." llathia trailed off and hung her head. "I'm sorry."

"For what? For doing your job?"

"Tashi told me only nobles are allowed to physically punish someone."

"The stories say he threatened you." Tzoca leaned forward and put his forehead against hers. "I didn't explain your position well enough. Roger took you under his care as a member of his household. That makes you, not quite family, but not a servant either. I took over his obligation when father sent him on his hunt. No one can touch you without your consent."

She reached up to him. "Do I give you permission?" Her hand caressed his cheek, leaving a dark smear behind. Tzoca stepped back as if she'd stabbed him.

"My apologies." His face darkened, in embarrassment or anger, she couldn't tell.

"I meant, my prince, you have my permission." Heat burned in her body, setting her hands to shaking, but she didn't lower her eyes.

"That would not be – wise." Tzoca sighed, his hand fluttered as if he wanted to reach for her again. "There are political considerations."

"I understand." Llathia pushed away from the tree. "You are a prince, and I, I don't know what I am." A sob tore from her throat and she scrambled away from him running away into the night.

Tzoca might have called something after her, but she didn't stop. Not until she stood on the edge of a high cliff. Lusundi was a deep pit, with tiny sparks of light here and there. Llathia gasped for air.

A strong arm encircled her waist and held her fast.

"I would regret it if you fell from this height." Chiza's voice buzzed against her back.

"I'm a fool, Chiza."

"Yes." Chiza said.

"You're supposed to argue." Llathia half laughed, half sobbed.

"We are all fools in the end."

"What am I supposed to do?"

"Work on your engine. Show it can be done. It will change us forever."

"Is that a good thing?" Ilathia held on to Chiza's arm. "What if we change the wrong way? What if we lose our heart?"

Chiza sighed. Llathia's heart beat slowed as she let herself feel safe here, with Chiza, at the edge of the world.

"What is our heart?" Chiza had an odd catch in his voice. "Is it love for the hunt? Most of the people in Lusundi no longer hunt. Is it reverence for the old ways? They are already changing."

"I think it is the desire to help the tribe. However we struggle for personal gain, if we remember we also serve the tribe, the nation…" Ilathia giggled. "Here I go explaining what you already know."

"What makes you think I know this?" Chiza's arm tightened. "I serve my Prince, because that is who I am. I never thought about why. Never thought there would be more to my life than that."

"I know how you feel." Llathia leaned her head back and squelched the sorrow she felt for the man who kept her safe.

They stood on the hill, the breeze blowing fitfully about them, then a voice called her name in the distance. Tashi, probably sent by the Prince to find her.

"Chiza promise me, if the time comes when you need to choose between me and doing what is right for the Congu, do what is right."

"I will try." Chiza sighed and carried her back from the edge before releasing his grip.

"We'd better go meet Tashi." Llathia walked away from the cliff, knowing Chiza would be behind her, loyal as her shadow.

***

The engine chugged as the pistons moved, then again, faster until the arms were a blur and the shaft spun at a scary speed. Her crew cheered and danced, some cried. Llathia hoped her father watched from the next life and was pleased with her work. Next would be the wheels and belts to transfer the power of the engine to whatever machine they built.

"A great achievement." Ntoox came up the hill to stand, hands on hips as if he owned the world. "You will make a good wife." He turned and stomped back down the hill, leaving llathia gasping as if he'd punched her in the gut.

Wife? Over my dead body.

Llathia forced the worry out of her head.

"Over here." She waved her arms. Her crew gathered around bubbling with excitement. Foresters, smiths, woodworkers, men and women who had shown up and begged to help.

"We have achieved the first step of our goal." Llathia shouted to be heard over the engine.

"First step?" Xinke shook his head. "She's running sweet as anything."

"Why?"

"Because you're the engine-smith, you made it happen."

"No, I mean, to what purpose?" Llathia pointed at the engine. "It runs, but out here in the middle of a field, what use is it? What are we going to do with the power?"

"Your dad ran a lumber mill." One of the foresters said.

"He did, but do you want to haul the logs up here to cut them? Or build the mill near the edge of the forest?"

"I can see using the power to work metal. The machine would be able to strike harder than a hammer. We already haul material up to the First Prince's Kraal, this isn't that much further."

Llathia saw heads nodding around her.

"Right then, we built a smithy here. Start thinking about what we need and how to use the power of the engine to run it. For now, rake out the fire, and let the pressure run itself off. For the next one we'll want a manual release. After it's stopped, grease everything that moves."

"The next one?" Xinke blinked.

"Don't you want that sawmill?" Llathia grinned. "If we can build them different sizes, they can run a pump to move water. I'm sure we'll think of more uses. The Anglians have engines on ships, you've seen them in the port. What is to stop us from doing the same?"

The men and women scattered, so llathia walked down the hill. Where before she'd never thought of Chiza's presence, now she was aware of him all the time, as if he'd become part of her body. She didn't know what to think about that. It was different from how Tzoca made her feel, entranced and frustrated both. She needed to talk to Tashi, but Chiza was always close by. The baths in the First Prince's Kraal had only a wall separating them from the hall.

How do I convince Tashi to take me to bathe in the Staal?

While Tashi scrubbed at the grease on llathia, she muttered that llathia must do it on purpose.

"I can't help it." Llathia winced as Tashi's fingers dug in. "If I'm going to work on the engine, I'm going to get greasy."

"Let the men work on it."

"What's the fun in that?" Llathia said.

Tashi shook llathia.

"It isn't a game, princess," she hissed. "Forces are moving you know nothing about."

"Ntoox." Llathia's pleasure evaporated.

"Him, he's the least of your worries right now."

"What?"

"Not here, it isn't safe."

"What about the bath in the Staal?"

"Dangerous, we'd put ourselves in Ntoox's path." Tashi growled. "If we are too obvious about being private, it will only make things worse.

"Can you read and write, Tashi?"

"The Prince insisted I learn."

"Very well. I believe I need to work on some drawing for the machinery to go with the engine."

From the feel of Tashi's fingers on her scalp, the maid didn't like the idea.

She didn't protest when llathia took out the paper and pencils.

What's this about?

Tzoca. Tashi's writing was blocky, but readable.

What about him?

There are rumours that you and him are lovers. It would be dishonourable. You are not a servant.

It's ok for him and a servant?

A servant has the right to refuse, but then where would she sleep? How would she eat? Tashi's pencil tore the paper.

Not Tzoca? Llathia tried to imagine him threatening Tashi.

Before. Tears spattered on the paper. *He came to visit our headsman. I worked in the house. Even then I was determined to be the best of maids. He threatened me, told me he'd destroy the headsman, make my family into beggars. When he left, I kept it a secret until the baby started showing. I couldn't explain. I was still afraid, but the headsman was wise and suspected. My daughter lives with my sister. I see her once a year, the rest of the time, I work here, keeping my secret.*

Does he know?

He can't know, she's still alive. He steals any boys, kills the girls. What can we do against him?

I will destroy him.

Llathia tore the paper into shreds, then dropped in them into the chamber pot, and poured water over them.

"Tashi, please empty the pot, I don't want to be smelling it all night."

Tashi left after composing her face. She came back, shoved the pot into its cubby and pointed to the bed.

"Time to sleep, mistress."

***

The work on the smithy progressed. They made wheels from rounds of wood, belts from woven rope. She tried to remember how her father had controlled speed. He'd talked about a balance between speed and power. Bh'ob spent hours discussing the shape of machines he wanted. The first was a mill to roll steel without using manpower to turn the massive cylinders of stone. Llathia built the largest wheel she could to run off the engine shaft and ran the belt to a much smaller one, even then the belt slipped. It was Bh'ob's idea to put teeth on the wheels and the belt.

Llathia also supervised the foresters as they started work on their own engine. She tried to hold back, let them show what they'd learned. There wasn't much she needed to remind them of. They even added things she wished she'd thought of. The feeling she'd reached the limit of what her father had taught her haunted her dreams, but no one accused her of lacking knowledge. From the process of building the engine, she moved to talking of the process of testing, failing and trying something different. Her father's favourite stories were all about moments he'd solved a difficult problem.

Since she worked down the hill as often as up, she and Tashi were moved back to their room in the Staal. The maid's face had lost its glow and she rarely smiled, as if telling Ilathia her story made it impossible to hide her pain.

The only blessing was the privacy they had in the baths. They lay in the pool and whispered. Oddly, they never talked about Tashi's story, or Ilathia's worries about Chiza. Instead Tashi would fill Ilathia in on the latest gossip, much of it about the engine-smith. To some she was a miracle worker and a blessing, but others feared what she achieved and wanted her stopped.

Rumours about her and Tzoca swirled about too. Llathia made sure to be polite and neutral around him. His eyes showed his puzzlement at first, then he returned her coolness. The more she play-acted that she didn't care for the Second Prince, the worse her heart ached over him.

Nothing came up about Ntoox, either because Tashi couldn't bear to talk about him, or there really was nothing to be said. Llathia wasn't about to ask.

Then the evening after the forester's engine ran successfully, the same middle-aged woman appeared to call llathia to a meeting with the First Wife.

Tashi coerced llathia into wearing something other than work clothes, then let her be led away. They wove through the hallways until once again, Chiza had to wait outside the door. Llathia didn't peek at any of the paintings or sculptures, she wanted a clear head.

"Leave us." The First Wife dismissed the women who buzzed around her. One of them llathia thought looked like Roger, but she was gone before llathia could be sure.

"Have you thought about marriage?" The First Wife studied llathia coldly.

"No, I've been too busy with my work." Llathia hoped her racing heart didn't give her away.

"Have you been sleeping with my son, trying to snare him into marriage?"

"No! First Wife. He is my Prince. It isn't my place to..." llathia's face burned.

"He says the same thing, but whatever the truth, wagging tongues will cause damage to our honour."

"If I may be so bold, who would question your family's honour on this?"

"Mtuaka." The First Wife spat out the name as if it pained her to speak it. "And that heir."

"The same heir known for leaving pregnant and weeping serving girls behind wherever he visits."

"It would be best if you never spoke of that. He is heir to the Mtuaka. Beyond some servant's prattle."

"I'm not just a servant." Llathia almost shouted, and the First Wife smiled.

"Finally, you begin to wake up and look about you. There is much more to the world than engines, however wondrous they are. If you aren't a servant, then I suggest you stop acting like one. The Mtuaka would like nothing more than to have their own engine-smith, and an offer of marriage would be hard to refuse. The old bull is up to something, he's too smug, but he's also an old hand at the game and we won't know his plan until it is too late to stop."

"So if I were to marry someone else…" Llathia thought of Chiza, she could do worse.

"Too late for that. They've spread their net and you wandered blindly into the center of it."

"Then what do I do?" llathia wailed. "I don't know this game you talk about. I never left my home until Roger dragged me away. Then he left me alone."

"Not quite alone." The First Wife's words hit llathia like a slap in the face. *I am a fool.* "I hear you, First Wife."

"I hope so, for all our sakes." The First Wife turned away, so llathia saluted, then picked her way out to the hall for the woman to return her to her room.

A tray of food sat in the corner. Llathia had no appetite, so she left it untouched. Tashi slept on her mat, the young woman had to be exhausted living under the same roof as the beast who had used her then thrown her away.

Llathia fell onto the bed, too tired to worry about her clothes. Let Tashi yell at her in the morning.

She didn't know what woke her. A noise where there shouldn't be one. The curtain rustling. Tashi wouldn't leave llathia alone. The woman's breathing sounded evenly from the other side of the room. Llathia rolled off her bed and crawled toward the lantern Tashi kept lit and hooded in case her mistress needed her.

Why isn't she awake? A foot scraped against the floor and llathia's skin crawled. There were people who be delighted if she died in the night. She changed direction and found the curtain covering the food laid out for her convenience.

Light blinded her, and her eyes watered.

"I was told you'd be asleep." Ntoox leered at her. "But this will be more fun." He crept toward her like a lion stalking his prey.

Llathia's hand closed around the knife. A tiny thing, a blade hardly longer than her finger. Her blood screamed at her to run, but that's what he wanted. A frightened girl, someone to use. Rage replaced the fear and she wished her stick was nearby.

He lunged at her, grabbing her dress and tearing it. She brought the knife around and slashed his face. Llathia didn't know she was screaming curses at him as she attacked until guards came and dragged her off him.

"Kill him," one of the them whispered.

"What?" Ilathia stared at the bleeding man lying moaning on the floor.

Other men pushed their way into the room. They glared at the guards, then one of them seized Ilathia.

"We're going to hold her. If our lord dies, she will die." He slung her over his shoulder and carried her out of the room.

Chapter 9 Snared

Roger pulled the canoe over to the shore and climbed out. He ached all over from crouching in the thing for days. There were too many villages along the shore, too many fishing boats. He looked like the enemy. Not everyone would give him time to explain.

The night was just about done, the sky lightened ahead of and already the sounds of people rising and going to work carried to him on the still air. The land here looked like someone had mixed the jungle and the plain together. Strings and clumps of trees dotted a landscape designed for cattle. The beasts were sleek and fat, mostly too lazy to do more than moo at him as he passed. The farmers weren't Sombi. Kershians walked the fields admiring their property, giving angry orders to the Sombi who used to live on the land. Roger had to restrain himself from killing the Kershians as he went, but he refused to let himself become a murderer. Slaughter was not the way of the hunt.

Clusters of houses where trails crossed grew to villages. The trees grew further apart, and stalking became harder. Even moving in the dead of night, dogs barked, and people shouted. And if they caught him at night, he was dead, even if it wasn't the Kershians who caught him.

He found the answer in a village where a tall man strode through the market wearing flowing robes, and more to Roger's advantage, a headdress which covered all but his eyes. Roger followed the man out of the village to a caravan of camels and horses.

"If you are going to stalk my master, you may as well come answer his questions." The point of a knife poking at his ribs made the suggestion into an order.

Roger walked calmly into the camp. There was no chance but to hope the man would understand and honour the idea of a herald. When they reached the fire, the hand with the knife travelled up to Roger's throat.

"Sit." The order was spoken in terse Sombi with an accent Roger couldn't identify. He lowered himself into a cross legged position and put his hands palm up. Someone took his bundle away, and probably would search it.

"The knife in the centre of the bundle is a gift from my King to the King of the Sombi." Roger said in Sombi.

"It's all right, Hillash, I doubt he will be able to attack with you watching." The man in the robes sat himself gracefully across the flames from Roger. His features looked chiselled from stone, but a smile softened the effect.

"I am sorry to cause you concern." Roger bowed in his sitting position. "I was trying to decide how to speak to you."

"Walking into camp and asking to talk to me wouldn't work?"

"Without knowing where you stood, it would be foolish."

"Where I stand? You make it sound like there is a war happening, but everywhere I look is peace."

"Peace for the Kershians, perhaps." Roger couldn't erase the bitterness from his voice. "In the grasslands and the jungle people die for the Kershian's sport."

"The tribe in that region are rebellious, I'm told. King vvatha asked the Kershians to help him restore order."

Roger laughed as tears ran down his cheeks.

"I've walked those paths and listened to the people. They didn't appear rebellious to me, unless it is rebellious to want to live. I've heard Kershians curse the people and call them beasts and slaves. Sometime in the near future, the King will die, and his daughter will be placed on the throne. Then the Kershians will do as they please."

"How do you know this? Do you speak Kershian? Maybe Anglian too. They have their own plans."

"The Empire plans nothing less than to rule the world." Roger said in Kershian. "The Anglians are oblivious to any danger not threatening their borders." This time he spoke in Anglian.

"Ah," the man spoke something in a fluid language, then cocked his head. "It is too much to hope that you'd speak the language of the desert."

"Perhaps someday I will have the opportunity to learn."

"I pray you do, Roger, Third Prince of Congu, but I do not see how you can survive here. There is an order to shoot Congu on sight. A private told a tale of ruthless Congu slaughtering a car load of unarmed soldiers."

"Guns are easy to hide." Roger sighed. "I did not wish to start a war, but it seems I am being given little choice."

The man leaned forward and spoke softly in Anglian.

"You killed a troop of Kershian soldiers?" The expression on his face looked more like hope than doubt.

"They are human and bleed. If you don't rush headlong into their weapons, they can be defeated.

144

War is changing. It is not hand to hand anymore but killing enemies one can barely see."

"There is talk of ships floating in the air," the man said. "What if they could drop stones on our heads?"

"The Kershians are not gods. Their technology gives them an advantage, so we meet their technology with our own."

"Your own?" The man leaned back. "And what is stop the Congu taking the place of the Kershians?"

"We hunt what we need and no more." Roger frowned. "What need do we have to rule our enemies? We would become soft and lazy, or hard and cruel."

"I will think on this. I'm sorry but I must insist you accept our hospitality tonight. The cold edge of Hillash's blade touched Roger's neck.

"I would be honoured."

They put him in a tent, hands tied to men on either side of him. In the morning, the man from the fire came to crouch down in front of him.

"My head says you are dangerous. The Kershians would thank me for giving them your body. But my heart weeps and pleads that you may be our hope. A year ago, our Omriph, King in your language died. An accident, sad, but they happen. His son is young and weak. There are voices whispering in his ears which say nothing good for my people." He sliced the ropes binding Roger. "I have always been one to trust my heart. What do you need of me? I will give you whatever aid I can, without revealing myself."

"Give me a set of your robes, white if you can. Teach me a few phrases of your language, then go on and forget you met me." Roger pulled the rope from his wrists. "You may want to remember some of my words in your dreams."

"There are so many Kershians, how can we rid ourselves of all of them?"

"You can't, we can't." Roger sighed and bowed his head. "To slaughter them would make us greater devils than they are. It is the leaders. Like an ant colony, kill the queen and the rest will run in disarray and listen to the first firm voice they hear. Especially if the words are not threatening."

"In my time in Anglia I learned that we cannot shut out the world, we choose how to take part, or it will be decided for us. I would not have our first decisions show us to be monsters."

"Where does one so young come upon such wisdom?"

"Wisdom?" Roger laughed and held up his hands. "I am not wise. I am terrified of making the wrong choice. It would be so easy to become a monster."

"If only more rulers shared your lack of wisdom." The man clapped his hands. "Hillash, ready clothes for the prince. Help him wear them properly." He peered at Roger. "Our language is beautiful even in the way we curse. Here is how to tell someone they are lower than camel dung."

Roger walked away from the camp, leading a horse. A bewildering array of curses circled in his mind. He'd insisted the man teach him a blessing or two to balance them. The robes were cool, people looked at him curiously, but they saw a desert man, not a Congu. Roger had left behind everything but the knife he meant as a gift and the water from the grass people. He wasn't sure why he kept it, but he couldn't bear to leave it behind.

He rode part of the day. Hillash's instructions on how to act, to sit, to talk echoed in his head. Roger hoped he didn't meet anyone familiar with the desert nation, or worse, spoke the language.

Biafa spread out in front of him the walls extending in either direction. Since the city was built on a plain, the Sombi had made their buildings into mountains. Several great pyramids lifted high above the wall tiny looking palaces sat atop them.

The warriors at the gate were Sombi, but Kershian soldiers lazed about not far from the gate, their deadly guns close at hand.

Roger walked through with little trouble, he needed to find ddokna's cousin. A butcher named zzilfa. It had seemed easier standing in the tall grass.

Just as Lusundi had poorer people near the harbour and wealthy high on the hill, Biafa showed its division between rich and poor. Roger didn't think the butcher would be wealthy. He wandered deeper into the city, turning toward the poor, but trying to avoid the destitute.

When the smell of death assaulted his nose, Roger turned toward it. He would learn about butchers near where animals were slaughtered.

He began asking, saying he'd been promised zzilfa could procure meat he'd be allowed to eat. Hillash ordered him to refrain from any meat. No desert person would eat flesh from an improperly killed animal. People looked at him and shrugged. One pointed randomly to one side. Roger followed the direction thinking they were as good as anything.

To his surprise, he met someone who knew zzilfa and directed him carefully to find the man's shop. Inside, Roger told the man that ddokna had sent him. The man paled and hurried Roger into the back room.

"What is he doing sending you here?" zzilfa hissed at him. "Does he want to get me killed? I'm already suspect coming from the riverlands."

"I didn't realize the Kershians were running the city."

Zzilfa laughed bitterly.

"Not the Kershians, but our own King who laps up the words of the Kershians like a dog at vomit."

Roger tried out a few of the curses the desert man had taught him.

"I was hoping King vvatha would at least give me a hearing."

"Not likely. He has his own plans for Congu, and they don't include the Xanachi."

"I've heard hints from the Kershians." Roger paced in the small room.

"Is it true? Have the river lands rebelled against the King?" zzilfa's face crumpled, Roger didn't know if the man wanted the answer to be yes or no.

"They are not happy with the Kershians."

"That is rebellion against the King." A voice spoke behind him. Roger spread his hands and lifted them away from his body.

"I hope you find peace." Roger said to zzilfa. "I hold no malice against you."

"How sweet. Turn around." The voice behind him dripped sarcasm.

Roger obeyed, keeping his face blank and his hands steady.

"You will find a knife wrapped in cloth in my belt on my right side. It is a gift for the King from his brother." The warrior claimed the knife and stuffed it in his belt without looking at it.

"And who would you be to be carrying gifts for the King?" The man had his hand near his sword as if Roger's answer could cause violence.

"I am Roger Hrona Xanachi, Third Prince of Congu." He nodded his head instead of saluting.

"We take him in and treat him like he's not lying. It's easy enough to beat him later."

"I promise to give you no trouble, but if there is a reward for my capture, I would ask that you give it to zzilfa as promised."

"You are the strangest prisoner I've ever taken." The man tossed a small bag to zzilfa. "Stay out of trouble, butcher." He pointed to the door and Roger walked ahead of him through the shop to the street where another six warriors waited. The man whistled and an answer came from the other side of the shop.

"I'm flattered that you think I am so dangerous. My brothers are the true warriors in the family."

"We heard about the train." The man pushed Roger into motion. "I wasn't risking any of my men." A warrior searched him thoroughly and lifted the rope with the gourds.

"What is this?"

"Water." The warrior shook it and shrugged, he slung it over his shoulder and walked away. Another warrior nudged Roger. He nodded and followed the men in front of him. They wound through the city to a grey stone building. A warrior opened the door, walked Roger to a cell and pushed him in. The door boomed shut behind him, a bar dropped into place. The footsteps of the warriors receded until Roger was left alone in silence.

Chapter 10 A Path at Night

Footsteps approaching the door woke Roger. He sat up and waited. When the door crashed open the light blinded him. Rough hands dragged him out of the cell and walked him to a room. They tied him to a chair, both hand and foot, removed the headdress, then left him alone his back to the door, facing a table.

New footsteps approached, heavier, more assured. When they entered the room, Roger sighed.

"I would salute properly, but I am prevented."

The footsteps moved around to where Roger could see the man. He had the same presence as his father. The same assurance of power. This man had gold rings on his fingers instead of scars on his body, but they sent the same message.

"My Captain told me who you claimed to be." King vvatha peered at Roger. "I didn't believe him." He dropped the knife and the gourds on the table. "Explain these."

"The knife is work by our bladesmith. I believe it to be equal in quality to the knives the traders bring. Perhaps not as good as the ones they keep for themselves."

King vvatha picked up the knife and pulled it from the sheath. He tested the edge and raised a brow. "I will accept this gift." He replaced it in the sheath and stuck it in his belt. "Now tell me why you are carrying water from the grass people. I am familiar with its effect."

"To be honest, I'm not sure why I've brought them. Perhaps for a time when it became important to hear the truth."

"A warrior who knows they are drinking the water can fight the effects."

"I don't need it." Roger dropped his head for a moment. "I have no reason to lie. I have no threats to move you, or promises to bribe you."

"Then why are you here?" The King leaned down to glare into Roger's eyes.

"My father thought it wise that I speak to you, his voice to your voice."

"He sent you as a herald?" The King spun and slammed his hand into the table. "Does he hate you that much?"

"If he sent someone else, the conversation would be different."

"You will die, and very shortly, your father and all his family will die."

"I suspected something like that when village warriors complained that Mtuaka wouldn't give them guns, as if they were sure he had them to give. Where would he get such weapons but from you?"

"Your father can't stand against Mtuaka, he has fifty warriors with rifles."

"You don't sound happy about that."

The King slammed the table again. "Mtuaka is a beast, his heir is worse. The stench of their slime will haunt me. But I will rule Congu."

"Why do you need to rule Congu?"

"You are enemies, I will put an end to the war."

"A little raiding, name calling across the river. We lived as peaceable enemies until the Kershians arrived. Their desire to rule the world is infectious."

"Don't tell me if you had the chance to take Sombi, that you wouldn't?"

"I hope I would not, I wouldn't know how to rule Sombi. They would make as poor Congu as we would make Sombi."

"Or desert man." The King paced about. "Why are you dressed as one?"

"Your warriors were looking for a Congu, not a desert man."

"You hoped to get close enough to me to assassinate me." The King slapped Roger.

"I am not the one plotting your death." He spit out blood.

"What?" King vvatha went still as a statue, only trembling in his hands betrayed him.

"I heard from the Kershian Colonel on the train. They plan to kill you and put your daughter in your place as a more tractable ruler."

King vvatha roared with laughter. "They underestimate my daughter." He took Roger by the throat.

"They did the same thing to the desert people a year past." Roger croaked

"How do I know you aren't lying?"

Roger pointed the gourds with his chin. The King loosened his grip and sagged against the table.

"I'd feared something like this. They always sound so reasonable, so earnest, but every time we talk, I've given away more of my country. Most of their soldiers have taken the train south to the river. They have guns and weapons which give me nightmares. My people will be slaughtered and to what purpose?"

"My King," Roger took a deep breath held it, then offered his words in place of an embrace. "Your people are loyal to you. They are ready for the

Kershians. Trust them. In the meantime, their numbers in Biafa are greatly reduced."

"They have a gunship in the harbour. It worth a thousand warriors."

"They are like ants. They need a queen to tell them what to do, while they hesitate, take the ship for your own. Aim at the head."

"I am going to hand you over to the Kershians." King vvatha looked grey and worn. "Make your peace." He picked up the gourds and left.

No one came for Roger. His arms and legs cramped and twisted. Itches tormented him. He tried to find a place where he could come to terms with his fate.

He failed.

He raged at his father who sent him to die. At the fates, which showed him so much of the world then were going to take it away. There was so much he wanted to do. Marry, have an heir, teach them to hunt with honour.

Tears flowed from his eyes and soaked his robes. The world was a horrible place, cruel and capricious. Why did he deserve this?

The door banged open and Kershian soldiers sneered at him as they dragged him away.

They kicked the door open at the top of the long climb and threw him into a room full of warriors wearing gilt armbands and on their fingers. Some made the King's handful of rings look restrained. None wore any weapons. King vvatha slouched on his throne, looking not at all happy.

The Kershians wore no gold beyond their rank symbols. An army's worth of officers gathered in the room. They laughed at Roger, making jokes in Kershian at his expense. Laughing at the King.

"Father." The strident voice belonged to a tiny empress. Gold cloth hung off her and scraped the floor. Gold combs competed for space in her hair. Her eyes flashed fire. She had no fear of her father or the Kershians. The King's daughter. His youngest, a blessing from his youngest wife. Or so people said until she started running the kingdom. Even in Congu people joked about the tiny girl who terrified her father.

"Father." She stomped over to his throne. "Is this how we treat guests? He may be Congu, he may be an enemy, but we are better than this." The girl didn't wait for an answer, but pointed to a warrior. "Get him something proper to wear." He looked uncertainly between the girl and her father who had his head in his hands. The warrior sighed and signalled to a servant and gave a quick order.

"You." She pointed to a servant. "Bring a pitcher of water and a basin." The servant didn't hesitate. Next, she came over to Roger. "Untie him." The Kershians looked down their noses at him. "Cowards, even with him bound, you shake in fear." The soldiers frowned, their faces darkening.

"Release him." The order came from the Khirsan who, if Roger read his uniform right, was a general as well as nobility. The man glared at the girl like he might an insect on his plate.

The servant returned with pitcher and basin.

"Wash yourself. You're going to die, die as a prince."

Roger tried to get his arms and legs to work, but they refused. Every effort embarrassed him further.

"My Queen, I beg your forgiveness." He closed his eyes and let his head drop to the floor.

"Oh for…" A cloth scrubbed his face. There was nothing gentle in it, but this child in gold washed his face. He opened his eyes and stared up into hers. Fire burned on the surface, beneath it, she shook with fear.

"My Queen." Roger whispered and gritting his teeth he wrenched his limbs into action until he knelt before her. "I will remember this kindness the rest of my life."

The Kershians broke into loud laughter. The girl frowned and clenched her fists.

"It will be all right." Roger said softly. She looked at him and shook her head, then ran from the room.

The servant arrived with clothes. He dispassionately removed the robes and helped Roger dress in the Sombi clothes as the Kershians laughed and jeered. The King sank further into his seat.

When Roger was able to stand on his own, dressed and clean. The general marched over to the King.

"This is all very amusing, but it doesn't befit a proper court." He pointed at Roger. "You must make an example of him to suppress the rebellion."

"I understand," the King sighed and sat himself straight. "I know you like the spirit we make from honey." He lifted a bottle and broke the seal, pouring some into large cups. Then he poured water into them. "Let us toast the end of our enemies." The King took a long sip of his drink.

The general made a sour face, then gulped down the liquid in his cup. He shook his head and threw the cup across the room.

"Disgusting stuff, I don't know how you savages can drink it. When we run the place, we'll bring in proper wine."

The warriors and the Kershians stared at the general, the first with growing anger, the others with worry.

"That brat will never do as a ruler; we'd be better slitting her throat." The general leaned toward the King. "She's a monster." Spittle splashed the King's face.

"My brother sent me a gift." The King spoke so quietly the people in the room stilled to hear his words. "Let me show you."

Roger couldn't see the thrust, but the general grunted then staggered back, red blossoming on the breast of his uniform. The King stood, panting, blood dripping from the knife in his hand.

A Kershian shouted something, it might have been an order to attack. They must have thought unarmed warriors would be weak.

The warriors didn't need weapons. They may have been fat and covered with gold and gems, but they swarmed the Kershians. Not one made it out the room alive.

King vvacha walked over to Roger and put his hand on Roger's shoulder.

"Take what men you need and capture that gunboat." He grinned broadly. "It was your idea."

"I want the men who brought me in."

"ssyache." The King nodded at a warrior. "He'll be in the barracks. Bring him. The rest of you. Take care of the Kershians. Give them a chance to surrender before you kill them. We are warriors."

The warriors ran out of the room in different directions. The King bent and pulled a pistol from the belt of the general.

"You know how to use this?"

"I do." Roger said.

"Take it." King vvacha pushed it into his hands. "I have the feeling you will need it."

Ssyache ran in with his squad and saluted the King.

"You and this man are going to capture the gunboat in the harbour." The King pointed at Roger.

"Why not?" ssyache saluted Roger. "What's the plan?"

"I'll explain it on the way to the docks."

The King heaved a sigh.

"Now that you've been given the easy task, I must go talk to my daughter."

***

Llathia lay in the cell. Mtuaka's warriors hadn't quite beaten her, but they'd made no attempt to be gentle. Bruises ached, a stabbing pain in her hand hinted at a broken finger at least. She was still covered with Ntoox's blood.

She hoped he survived, not because she cared about him, but because she didn't want to be a killer.

Shouting sounded outside the room. It ebbed and flowed as if people came and left the argument. Llathia couldn't make out any words. Her head didn't feel right. Easier to lie here and wait for fate to flip its coin to let her live or die.

The door opened and warriors pushed a ball of fury into the room. Tashi rounded on them. "I need water and bandages." The door slammed and the bar dropped into place. All the energy left Tashi and she collapsed beside llathia. "I'm sorry, my princess." Sobs shook her until llathia feared she'd come apart. The hand without the broken bones agreed to move, a little, enough to touch Tashi on the head.

"They drugged you, I hate to think of what they did to Chiza."

"He lives, barely." Tashi ground her teeth. "The dogs."

"The First Wife told me to stop acting like a servant." Llathia let out a single laugh, then groaned as pain shot through her ribs. "I don't think this is what she had in mind."

"What happened? I woke in the room alone with blood all over." Tashi jerked her head up. "You must be terribly wounded." She started to tear at her uniform.

"Not my blood." Llathia said. Her hand trembled as she remembered the rage. "Ntoox planned to take me while I slept. I used the fruit knife. They weren't sure if he'd live."

"Ntoox?" Tashi stared at llathia as if she'd grown another head. "You may have killed Ntoox?" Tashi howled in rage, but didn't move from under llathia's hand. "I have dreamed of killing him, dreams so real I woke shaking." She kissed llathia's broken hand. "You are my princess. I will serve you for the rest of my life."

"I'd rather he didn't die," llathia said. "I don't want to be a murderer. The guard wanted me to kill him."

"If he lives, he can demand your life. You've assaulted a noble."

"I'm not afraid to die."

"No." Tashi shook her head under Llathia's hand. "He can make you his slave. Force you into his bed, whatever he wants with no restraint."

"If he dies?"

"If he'd died in your room you could have claimed self-defence. You aren't quite a noble, but you are more than a servant. Especially since they drugged Chiza and me. If he dies now." Tashi let out a sob. "They will kill you. Mtuaka has claimed right of judgement because of the injury to his heir."

"He is treating me as a servant then." Llathia tried to sit up, but the room spun around her and she fell back on the bed.

"Your head is bleeding." Tashi probed it gently. "Did he hit you?"

"No, I think they banged it throwing me into this room. It's hard to remember. He grabbed my dress, tore it, then everything is blurry, like I'm looking through water." Llathia closed her eyes.

"Mistress, princess." Tashi shook her. "Llathia, you can't sleep. Talk to me."

"How do I act so they don't treat me like a servant?"

"A servant has no rights against a noble. They can rape and murder us and all we can do is die."

"If I'm not a servant, I get a trial. I get to plead in front of the King?"

"I guess, I can't remember a noble ever being tried, but you aren't a noble, you can't involve the King. He'll kill you to shut up Mtuaka."

"What happens if Tzoca has a grievance against Mtuaka?"

"They fight, or their champions fight, depending on the grievance. One of them dies. It happened a few years back. An heir refused to let Mtuaka wed his sister, even after the agreement had been signed."

"So he had to fight Mtuaka?"

"No, it would have been his father. It was his father's word he rebelled against."

"He had to kill his father to save his sister?" The horror washed some of the pain and fog from Ilathia's head.

"He refused. The King banished him and stripped him of everything but his use name. If he returns, anyone who sees him must kill him, or at least die trying."

"Then I will challenge Ntoox to a fight." Llathia giggled. The notion of her going up against the big man was ridiculous.

"Are you insane?" Tashi cried. "You won't catch him by surprise again. He'd destroy you."

"But I'd be dead, not his slave."

"You are insane. It's your head, you're not thinking right."

"Even if you're right, what other choice do I have?"

"The Prince will do something, let him help you."

"If he takes action to protect me, then he's open to being challenged as being responsible for my action. He'd have to fight. Can I let him fight Ntoox for my crime?"

"He'll want to." Tashi said. "He…"

"I can't let him." Llathia didn't know why she knew that. What had the First Wife said? Her head was filled with fluff.

There were noises outside the room again. Shouting and crashing, then the door blew open, breaking against the wall and twisting off one hinge. Ntoox stood in the door. Bandages covered his face and hands.

"I'm going to kill you."

"You can't," a warrior pleaded trying to drag Ntoox away. "Mtuaka said—"

"She can't attack my honour and live." Ntoox slammed his fist into the warrior's face sending him to the floor. The big man stepped into the room. "Now I'm going to finish what I started."

A large hand gripped Ntoox's neck and pulled him back.

"Don't force me to kill you. For some reason, the King wants you alive." Chiza stood between Ntoox and llathia.

"I'll kill you too." Ntoox roared.

"Then come on." Chiza lifted his hands. "Kill me."

"Nobody's killing anybody." The King stalked into the room, anger radiating from him. Ntoox backed away and Chiza saluted.

"Give me one reason I shouldn't hand you over to Mtuaka." The King's eyes bored into Ilathia. *He's asking* me *how? He's the King.* Pieces fell into place. Not all of them, but enough. Something had the King backed into a corner. This situation could shatter him or save him.

"I challenge Ntoox to a fight to the death." Llathia pointed at the man.

"What?" The shout came from three throats.

"Ntoox said I attacked his honour. The warrior on the floor heard him. A servant can't touch any honour but their masters by their actions. So Ntoox recognizes me as an equal."

Ntoox shouted incoherently and made as if to push past the King. Mtuaka stepped into the already crowded room and slapped Ntoox across the face.

"Out," he shouted. "You're an idiot. Get out of my sight before I disown you."

Ntoox deflated and stomped away.

"This woman," Mtuaka pointed at Ilathia. "Conspired against my heir to embarrass me." He faced the King shaking with rage. "She sent a note to Ntoox inviting him to her room promising to drug her maid and Right Arm to keep it quiet. He went, foolishly perhaps, expecting a chance to talk about marriage, though what he sees in her I don't know."

"Ilathia gave me no food."

"You're her Right Arm, and you love her. Of course you'd lie to protect her, even though she almost killed you."

The King raised his hand stilling Chiza's response.

"They will fight in three days. You are not to interfere." He turned to Ilathia and frowned. "When you lose, Ntoox's honour will be restored. Normally all your holdings would be forfeit, but you have none, so he'll have to be satisfied."

"And if I win?" Ilathia asked.

"You will not win against Ntoox." The King voice was flat and implacable.

"And if I win?" she asked again holding the King's gaze.

"If you win," the King snarled the words. "I will try you for conspiracy against Mtuaka. And unless you have a noble witness to refute his claim you will die for your crime."

He turned and walked out of the room, Mtuaka shrinking away from him.

"I will hold her here." Mtuaka said when the King had gone.

"Did you not hear the King?" Chiza crossed his arms. "They are to fight in the arena for Ntoox's honour. You have no right to hold another noble. She is honour bound to appear, or she forfeits. I will ensure she walks onto the sand prepared to shed blood." He stepped closer to Mtuaka. "Anyone who tries to interfere with her will die. That includes the warthog you claim as heir."

Mtuaka darkened, but he only slammed the wall and stormed cursing loudly out of the room.

"Can you walk?" Chiza looked down at Llathia, his face stone.

"I can." Llathia pushed to her feet, supported herself on Tashi's shoulder, then followed Chiza out of the room.

Chapter 11 The Dreadful Bargain

Roger led the Sombi warriors down to the dock.

"The gunboat will have maybe twelve people on board. Most of them will not be armed. Even the ones who work the gun won't have weapons of their own. The people we need to get to are the ones on the bridge. They will have weapons and can order the crew to use the gun against Biafa."

"How do we get to those people?"

"There will be a nightwatch, because there's always a nightwatch. They won't expect to see anything, much less have warriors attack their boat. These people are powerful because of their technology, but it is also their weakness. They depend on it too much."

"We take the nightwatch, then the bridge?"

"That and officer's quarters where the other people we need to control will be. We must be quick and silent. Don't kill if you don't need to, but don't hesitate if you must."

"Why should we spare our enemies?"

"Most of these men have no more choice about being here than you do. Their King orders them, and they go. Besides I think we will want some people in Locasia who can say we are more than savages."

At the dock, they found a boat and rowed out into the night black harbour. The gunboat a darker shape against the sky, except for one lantern illuminating a man leaning on the rail. The only movement was him occasionally spitting into the water.

The warriors climbed up the anchor chain. Two of them split off and headed toward the watchman. Roger lead the rest toward the bow. He climbed onto the top deck and crept along until he stood over a sailor standing guard by the bridge door. The man had a sidearm. Roger dropped on him wrapping his arm around the man's throat, pulling the gun as he crashed back through the door. Ssarche led his men up the stair and through the door as the sailor on the bridge stared in horror at the invaders.

"Officer's quarters." Roger pointed down the passageway. Muffled thumps and groans revealed the progress of the warriors. Ssarche returned.

"All secure." The blood dripping from his hand set the sailor to shaking.

"Take this man to the gun room." Roger ordered the sailor.

"Don't you dare help—" the man who'd guarded the door groaned and slumped to the floor. The warrior behind him cleaned his knife and returned it to his belt.

The remaining sailor showed the warriors to the gun room. Ssarche left a man guarding it, then the warriors went through the ship rousting out the sailors and bringing them to the back deck.

"You are now prisoner of the King of Sombi. If you behave you will be well treated."

"Forget that you dirty savage." A big man lunged at a warrior and wrested a knife from the Sombi. Roger shot him as he slashed at the warrior.

"Any other heroes?" The men knelt and put their hands on their head.

Roger had the warriors supervise a couple of sailors raising the anchor. The others were locked in the hold after Roger checked for anything that could be made into a weapon. It was slow work, but the warriors towed the gunboat to the dock where the King met them with a group of men. The King's daughter stood beside her father, scowling.

"Get the prisoners off my boat, lock them in the cells for now." The King watched as the men were marched off the ship. The bodies, they laid out on the wharf.

"We need to get underway." The King walked up the gangplank, followed by his men, some of them went down into the ship, others up to the bridge. "Not all of them were happy about being woken in the middle of the night." The King stood watching the activity on the deck. "But they are happy enough with what I'm paying them."

The gunboat was steaming south before the sun rose out of the ocean.

"Congu," The King's daughter came up and stood on her toes to see over the railing. "Did you mean what you said?"

"I generally try to." Roger waved a Sombi over. "Find a box for the King's daughter."

"I thought I was your queen." Her voice had a definite edge.

"You are my queen, but not his."

"Oh."

The man returned with a crate and set it by her. She climbed up on the box and leaned against the railing.

"Do you think I'm a monster?"

Roger glanced at her and saw tears shining on her cheeks.

"I think you are brave, and trying your best to make sense of a world that doesn't make much sense."

"But I'm mean, and I yell at people, and sometimes I call them terrible things."

"And sometimes you demand kindness toward a prisoner even when everyone laughs at you." Roger sighed. "Life is complicated."

"Look!" The King's daughter pointed out to sea where dolphins played in the light of the rising sun. "I wish I could be like that."

"What's stopping you?"

"I'm not a dolphin." She snapped at him with that edge in her voice again.

"No, listen." Roger closed his eyes. How to explain something he barely understood? "Those dolphins. They aren't worried about being anything other than dolphins. So they do what dolphins do, right now that means dancing for the King's daughter."

"Stop calling me that." She yelled at him. "My name is pponema kkitatin ssombi."

"I'm sorry. Which name would you like me to call you?"

"kkitatin." She said in a faraway voice. "It is a bird in the jungle. It's supposed to be the most beautiful bird anywhere. Everyone else calls me princess, or King's Daughter or pponema, but you'll call me kkitatin."

"As you wish kkitakin." They watched the dolphins until they disappeared.

She went to find a room to rest in, commandeering a sailor as she walked past. Roger went looking for the King.

"I saw you were talking to pponema." King vvatha sighed. "She never really talks to me. I didn't know what to do with her. She's the youngest of all my children, but it's like she's an only child. The others are busy, and to be honest, just I avoid her."

"She's a girl trying to figure out how she fits in the world."

"Are we talking about the same girl?" The King shook his head. "I like you, you saved my life and my country. I'm in your debt. My son is working on setting things right, but it will never be the same. We need at least some of the Kershians, but we'll deal with them on our terms. They will obey our laws, but at the same time we want them to teach us how to use the things they've built. What was I saying?" The King stared out to see for a moment. "Right. I like you, but I don't understand you. It's like you live in a different world than I do."

"My father sent me on a mission. He would have known I would possibly die. When I was tied up in your prison, I hated him for that. It wasn't fair putting all that on my shoulders, what was I supposed to do? I've been making it up as I go, trying to think of peace. It's like I'm hunting an entirely new creature. I have no idea what I'm doing, but each time I get close, I learn something. Anyway, while I shouted and cried at my father, and life and the gods, I realized something." Roger looked out at the shore passing not as far from them as the other side of the river.

"So you realized something." The King's sarcasm nudged him. "What?"

"My father trusted me. Succeed or fail, even if I have no idea what I'm doing, I still speak with his voice. I just keep doing what I can to find the path."

"You don't make any sense at all." The King huffed, then walked away.

"Why are we here? What's the rush?" Roger stared at the passing shore. *I hope whatever Mtuaka is up to, I get there in time to stop it.* The King knew what Mtuaka was going to do. He'd helped plan it. Fifty rifles. Even with that they'd be hard pressed to defeat his father's warriors.

Roger thought about the Kershians. If his father and their family died, there would be no one to guide the warriors. Mtuaka would step into the vacuum. But he needed to get them all at once. King vvatha was rushing Roger home to be with his father. Was he still working to set up Mtuaka to rule Congu? He understood Mtuaka, even if he detested him, but he said himself, he didn't understand Roger. Even powerful men fear what they don't understand.

He stood at the rail turning over the possibilities in his head. He couldn't put it together.

"What are you doing?" kkitatin dropped the crate she was carrying beside Roger and stood on it to peer over the rail.

"Thinking."

"Father does a lot of that." She put her chin on her hands. "He's always trying to figure out if he can trust people. He says it's his job as King."

"Being King isn't easy. He has a lot of people to think about."

"Now you sound like him." Kkitatin pouted. "I liked you better when you were being a dolphin."

"Do you trust your father?"

"No, he lies to me all the time. He promises to spend time with me, just with me, then someone comes, and he says he has to be King. I don't have a father; I have a King. Sometimes I hate him."

"And the other times?"

"I wish he'd be a father I could love. I'm not even sure what that means." She sniffed and ran away.

Dolphins and Kings got mixed up in Roger's thinking. Kkitatin liked him as a dolphin. But he needed to be a herald, his King's voice.

"I've stopped speaking for my King." Roger shook his head. "I've let King vvacha take over. I need to start the conversation again, but he's not going to just let me." The headland appeared ahead. They'd make port soon.

Roger climbed up on the railing and dove into the water. It was cool, refreshing and buoyed him up.

He swam toward the shore. He and his brothers had covered longer distances when they were young. When he got to shore, he would find his father and explain how they could win this and set a new course for both Congu and Sombi.

***

The fog slowly lifted from Ilathia's mind. That was a problem. The more clearly she thought, the more terrified she felt. She'd challenged Ntoox to a death match. Ntoox, the man who only the King or Chiza could beat, maybe.

Tashi alternated between being cheerful and ranting at Ilathia. Chiza said nothing at all, even more closed off than he'd ever been. Llathia had grown used to feeling his warm presence at her back. It was still there but cold, as if only his duty to Roger kept him there. A dozen times a day, Ilathia thought of sending Chiza away, but then she imagined not having him there and changed her mind.

Now there was only one day before she walked out on the sand to die, and she wanted just for a little while to feel safe like she had on the edge of the cliff watching the night.

"Chiza." Llathia walked out into the foyer of her suite. They'd put her in rooms that made her original room look like a closet. He turned to look at her, then back to the door. "Nobody is going to come through the door. I need to talk to you."

He didn't move, more like a statue than a stone. Llathia moved around in front of him.

"Chiza. Look at me." Llathia struggled against tears. If she started, she'd never stop. Instead she dug in and fed her anger. She was tired of this. Tashi thinking she was going to die. Chiza acting like she was already dead. "Blast you. Look at me." She swung her fist at him, and he blocked it without even looking.

She kept punching, kicking, shouting. Chiza defended himself with no emotion. Llathia's rage overflowed, it burned her, lifted her up, built up pressure like her steam engine. All of it she aimed at Chiza, he had to move faster to avoid her blows and not injure her. Then he stepped back and back again. He frowned as he moved his hands in a blur, always faster than she could move.

"Hit back." She screamed it at him, needing to feel his anger, his hatred on her skin. Bruising her body like it bruised her soul. He refused. Stone, taking everything she threw at him, not needing anything else to defeat her.

There was only one thing she could try. Even in the fire of her anger she knew it would hurt. It could break her, leave her empty, already dead before she stepped on the sand.

Tears blinded her, but she didn't need to see. The chill of his hatred guided her. Her arms ached with the bruising from his blocks, each one perfect, exact. She lunged forward to head butt him. His elbow crashed into her forehead. Pain ran through her, but she rolled to her feet. Chiza finally saw her, an expression running across his face. Not hatred, not at all.

Her hand stung when it hit his face. He hadn't moved. She swung again, and his arms wrapped around her and held her still. Warmth eased the pain in her heart.

"Were you really going to let me go into battle without my Right Arm?" She spoke into his chest, muffled, straight to his heart. Something strange dripped onto her neck, then her shoulder. Llathia wrapped her arms as far as they could reach around him. "I need you." She whispered it, but he must have heard. He slackened his grip and tilted her head up with a finger. The mark of her hand stood out on his skin. Dark red against the bronze. His tears streamed endlessly from his eyes.

"Forgive me." Chiza went to his knees and put his head on her shoulders.

"Of course, I forgive you." She put her head against his. "You are part of me. I can't hate my own arm."

"I'm so afraid," Chiza whispered. "I'm not afraid to die, I've faced death a thousand times. But I'm afraid of losing you, of failing you."

"You can't fail me." Llathia hugged his neck. "Whatever happens tomorrow, you haven't failed me.

Promise you will go on, find Roger and take care of him."

"You asked me if I had to choose, to do what is right." Chiza choked on the words. "I don't know if I can. If I'm part of you, then you are part of me. I'm just an arm, you are heart and fire and mind."

He stood suddenly, then lifted her to her feet.

"Ntoox is strong, but he isn't smart. I'll teach you how to defeat him."

"Then there is the trial."

"Leave that part to me." Tashi peeked out through the curtain from the bedroom. "I have an idea. I'm going to go out and leave you alone for a while." She stressed the *alone*.

"You were going to teach me something?" Ilathia took what she thought a fighting stance would look like.

"That's not at all what I had in mind." Tashi shook her head and went out the door.

***

Roger pulled himself onto the balcony. He worked the door lock with his knife and pulled it open.

"You'd better have a good reason for disturbing me." King Xanachi growled from his bed.

"I do." Roger stepped into the room.

"Roger!" His father rolled out of bed and unhooded a lantern. "I thought it was one of your brothers. They've been harassing me about this whole engine-smith mess."

"Engine-smith mess?" Roger shook his head. "Let me fill you in, then you can explain the mess.

"Report."

Roger grinned. "How long have we been breaking into your room?"

"Since Bhansin learned to climb to the balcony."

"You really should have fixed the door lock." Roger pulled a chair over and sat down.

"I wouldn't get to visit with my sons then." The King tried to glower at Roger. "You were going to report?"

"Right. I'll start off with Mtuaka planning to take over using the fifty rifles he got from Sombi in exchange for his help."

"Fifty, huh?" The King scrubbed at his face. "I was hoping it would be only one or two."

"Did you get the message I sent?"

"You mean the endless line of village warriors demanding I give the guns?"

"Endless line?" Roger frowned. "I only sent one."

"And he talked to every village between here and the river."

"I didn't think of that."

"Clever though. They never got to talk to me in person of course. The warriors took their complaints and said they'd pass it on to me, and I would come up with a solution. A lot of them took up work of one kind or another while they're here."

"So Mtuaka has men with guns, and we have a lot of men who want them." Roger raised a brow.

"I think I see where you're going with this. It could work too. I look forward to the look on Mtuaka's face." The King grinned, and Roger was reminded again why his father was the most feared warrior in Congu. "What else have you been up to aside from that?"

"Well I should start with the Sombi village built on our side of the river…" Roger launched into his tale. His father alternated between sitting and pacing about the room. At a couple of places, he might have been brushing away tears.

"So that's pretty much it." Roger sighed, exhausted by reliving his journey. "I expect King vvacha will make an appearance soon, but I don't know what his game is. Which is why I came to talk to you."

"The gunboat moored at a dock, but we haven't heard anything from it yet. I'll make sure to send a suitable welcome committee. It will keep vvacha from getting into trouble. I doubt he knows what his game is. He's just like that, but he's a canny one." King Xanachi walked to the balcony and stared out over the city. "What's our game? What do you want out of this?"

"The Kershians have their fingers in Sombi, the desert kingdom west of them, in ours. The only way we can respond is if we show a united front."

"The Congu and Sombi will never unite, and that's just the two. There are dozens of countries across Harasah."

"We don't need to unite." Roger stood beside his father. "We're stronger with all our differences, but we could work together to address the Kershian threat. People from different countries who don't want to lose themselves to the Empire."

"A Harasah defense agreement." The King slapped Roger on the back making him grunt. "I like it, and if we play it right, vvacha will join and even believe it's his own idea."

"Now what is this about Ilathia?"

"She's challenged Ntoox to a death match. It's tomorrow." The King sighed and leaned on the balcony. "She's bright, and more to the point, she knows how to lead, but she hasn't got the political sense of a squash. Your report dropped the last few pieces in place. I'll be able to deal with Mtuaka once and for all."

"But Ntoox is going to kill her." Roger wanted to shake his father. "We have to stop it."

"I can't. It's Bundo all over again. If I get involved, then Mtuaka will have the leverage he needs to justify a coup." The King turned and put a hand on Roger's shoulder. "There's something about her. She slashed Ntoox's face when he attacked her in her room. The guards had to pull her away from him. If she can focus that, she might have a chance."

"I hope so." Roger hugged his father. "Thanks. Thank you for letting us claim some of your time. I recently learned how lucky I am." He climbed out over the balcony. "I'll be at the arena tomorrow. Maybe invite vvacha, he'd enjoy it."

Chapter 11   The Trap is Sprung

The sand burned her feet, but llathia welcomed the pain. It pushed away the fear. She held a spear in her right hand, a shield in her left. The sun beat down mercilessly. There was no shade in the arena. Spectators lined the stand. Murmurs echoed strangely. A woman in the arena, a woman against a warrior, one of the biggest, one of the best. Even Chiza feared him, maybe. It depended on who was talking.

"We are here to witness justice." The King's voice boomed across the arena, dry, sarcastic. Llathia knew he'd already buried her in his mind. She was a ghost. Llathia smiled. Even out here near the center of the huge space, Chiza's presence warmed her back. She was whole.

Live or die, she was content.

"The gods witness this conflict. Let the combatants state one last time their grievance."

"She conspired against me. Ambushed me. I will destroy her." Ntoox spread his arms and roared his complaint. The lines of his wounds were still fresh on his face.

"He is a rapist, a child killer, he's not fit to call himself Congu. Who hunts the helpless and can call himself a warrior? The man is a coward. I don't need to destroy him, he's already worthless."

With each word llathia built the pressure within her. She'd used it without thinking against the forester, then Ntoox. Chiza at the last, taught her to harness it. Her words were her first attack.

Ntoox screamed wordlessly and waved his spear, clanging it against his shield. Llathia waited until he had wound down enough to hear her.

"I've already beaten you once. Prepare to die, little man."

"Enough." The King's voice cracked across the arena. "Let's get this over with." He tossed a white cloth into the arena.

Llathia crouched behind her shield letting it rest on the sand. Ntoox's feet thudded against the sand as he charged. She stood still, spear held out to the right, left hand holding the shield, peeking around the edge just enough to watch her opponent.

He ran with his arm cocked back ready to throw. Then he planted his foot, not three paces away from her and threw his spear at her with all the strength in his body. It flashed through the air, hit her shield and blew through it like it was paper.

Llathia would have been dead if she'd remained behind the shield, but before his spear connected she was already moving.

When Ntoox made his mighty throw, he moved his left arm to keep his balance as if llathia posed no risk to him. It opened enough space for her spear to slide past his shield and between his ribs, driven by her fury and the last of his own forward momentum. She twisted to the side and shoved with all her strength. The point found his heart, then pushed through his back.

He was dead before he hit the ground.

The people in the stands froze, soundless, their breath snatched from them by shock, then one found their voice, then another until the ground shook with the noise. Llathia walked through it until she stood in front of the King.

"I believe that takes care of the accusation against me." Llathia spoke as if only her and the King were present.

"No." Mtuaka stood up and railed at the King. "She must still answer my complaint."

"I did say you would face my justice, engine-smith." The words sounded forced, as if the King fought to hold them back. "Unless you have a noble who will witness in your defence."

"I believe I might have something to say about that, husband." The First Wife stood and removed the veil which had hidden her face.

***

Roger stared at Ntoox, lying dead on the sand with Ilathia's spear through his heart. She walked up to face the King like a queen of legend. Then when First Wife spoke up, he nearly forgot what he was about. He wore a headcovering, bright red. It didn't fit well, so it hung over his face.

When First Wife stood, everyone fixed their eyes on her. Roger turned the other way and mopped at his face with a black cloth. Then he swivelled to watch the unfolding drama.

"The engine-smith was in my rooms at the time the maid and the Right Arm were drugged."

"Who could drug a Right Arm, but their master? Who else would he trust?" Mtuaka sputtered, his face darkening.

"That would be true if indeed he was fed drugged food." First Wife played with something in her hands. "There are a fascinating people who live in Sombi. Very different from us. They use blowguns to hunt, with poisoned darts which could kill a man, or render a very strong one unconscious, almost immediately. You wouldn't know any of that would you?"

Roger looked closer and recognized a blowgun from the grass people.

"I've never seen that before." Mtuaka pointed at the thing in First Wife's hands.

"Of course you haven't, how would you, loyal lord that you are. It was found in Ntoox's room. The poor boy is in no shape to defend himself, is he?"

"The woman threatened him. He showed me himself a piece of a letter saying she would destroy him. Perhaps he needed a subtle way of defending himself."

For some strange reason, Ilathia was shaking. Roger worried that she'd fallen into some trap, but then she put her head back and roared with laughter. Mtuaka shook with rage while the First Wife looked on with an elegantly raise eyebrow.

"Do explain your amusement, dear."

"My apologies, First Wife, my King, but the only way Ntoox could have found that bit of letter was by searching my chamber-pot." She snorted and fought visibly to control her laughter.

"Chamber-pot?" The eyebrow went higher.

"My maid and I conversed by writing on a paper. I closed the conversation by saying I would destroy Ntoox. I tore it up and threw it into the chamber pot, which my maid emptied. I never checked to be sure all the paper was gone. He must have found it after we were moved to First Prince's Kraal. But I don't understand why he would have been interested in the contents of a lady's chamber-pot in the first place."

A rustle went through the crowd as the people talked and laughed. Mtuaka had turned grey.

"Do we need to continue this?" First Wife looked over at the King. "I think it's clear who was conspiring against who."

"You witch, I'll see you dead." Mtuaka screamed and yanked a pistol out of his tunic. Roger raised the black cloth over his head, but it would be too slow.

The First Wife put the blowgun to her lips, then Mtuaka stumbled back batting at his neck. He fell and quivered once before going still.

"Mtuaka's warriors." The King shouted over the gasps and murmurs. "Anyone who attempts to use the guns you carry will die, just as your lord did. If you want to live, walk down onto the sand and place your gun on the ground."

Roger kept his hand with the cloth up until a warrior stood and moved onto the sand. He knelt and placed a gun on the ground before backing up and prostrating himself. Others moved too. One pulled out his rifle, but arrows from the archers lining the top of the stands turned him into corpse before he could aim. None of the other warriors resisted.

"Guards escort the prisoners to the cells, treat them as if they have given their bond."

The archers slackened their bows and watched as guards escorted the Mtuak warriors away.

***

Llathia watched the last of the warriors disappear under the stands, then she turned to salute the First Wife. The woman's mouth twitched into a smile and she saluted back with the blowgun.

"This was much more entertaining than I expected," King Xanachi said. He turned to someone who sat beside him on the stand.

"Indeed." The speaker was a heavy set man with gold rings on every finger. A girl beside him watched the proceedings with wide eyes.

"It appears I need a new leader for the Mtuak, since their lord and his heir have died."

"Doesn't a rebellious leader forfeit all their holdings to the King?" The man with the rings waved his hands as he talked.

"Probably, but I don't have time to deal with the Mtuak, they've always been fractious, maybe it's all the raiding back and forth over the river. Warriors start thinking about their reputation instead of how to serve their people." The King pointed at llathia. "Engine-smith, since you have been cleared of the accusations against you, by combat and by testimony. What do you demand in return for the attack on your honour and your person?"

Llathia's mind went blank. She'd not thought past surviving. What she wanted wasn't something the King could give her.

"I don't know, my King. Being alive to serve you is more than enough for now."

The King turned to the man with the rings and muttered something. The only word she could make out was *squash.* Llathia waited.

"First Wife, if I may have a word?" The King extended his hand. She glided over and took it briefly.

"How may I serve my King?" The First Wife's words were layered with meanings llathia couldn't understand, but from the expressions crossing the King's face, he got the message.

"My new leader of the Mtuak will need a political advisor. Could I impose on you to consider the position?"

"Is my King releasing me?" The First Wife's face stayed expressionless, giving llathia no clue about what the woman wanted.

"You will always be my First Wife, but whether you choose to leave or to stay in the woman's quarters, I will let you decide."

"Indeed." The slightest tinge of red crossed the polished bronze of her expression. "Then I will accept your request. It sounds amusing, and things here have been so dull lately." She waved her hand at the corpses on the sand.

"You have my gratitude." The King smiled and saluted his First Wife, then turned to glower at llathia. "I believe you were told to act more like a noble. Nobles always want something, even if it isn't good for them. You must learn. First Wife will aid you."

"But she's helping the new Mtua—" llathia stopped as it dawned on her what was going on. "My King, you can't."

"I have, and I've promised my First Wife some amusement. She is not a woman to allow a broken promise."

Llathia looked around desperately. Surely there was some way to escape. Then she caught the First Wife's expression. Pleading and sympathy mixed.

"My King, your servant, however unworthy, accepts your command." Llathia saluted him. The crowd burbled with excitement, then a woman's voice cheered, and the rest joined in.

When the noise had settled down, llathia tilted her head at the King. "I would like to choose my own staff."

"See," the King pointed to llathia while grinning at the First Wife. "She's learning already. Bring me a list at the banquet."

"Banquet?" Llathia's head started spinning.

"A welcome banquet for some visitors. Wear something suitable for the lady of the Mtuak." He raised his voice. "I hope you enjoyed today's events as much as I did. The Staal will be distributing food and drink in the lower square for all my people to enjoy."

The arena erupted in more cheers.

Tashi ran across the sand to embrace llathia. Chiza followed at a slower pace, but his smile said a great deal.

"I need your help with this dress." Llathia's heart pounded with mixed joy and terror. "What am I going to do?"

Chapter 12 Unexpected Plans

Llathia tried to move in the clothes Tashi had shoehorned her into.

"You don't stride around like a forester in this dress. Glide." Tashi had her hand on her chin, considering. "It needs a little more."

"More?" llathia's voice squeaked. She hadn't been this afraid facing Ntoox in the arena. Of course, there the worst that could happen was she'd die. At this banquet? She shuddered.

Tashi pinned something to the breast of llathia's wrap. A tiny gold pin, nobody would see with all the gaudy necklaces, rings and earings draped around her body. Still llathia's heart started to slow. She was the engine-smith still. All the trappings didn't change that. What could she do with the resources of the Mtuak?

"You're plotting." Tashi grinned at her. "Now you really do look like a noble."

"I'm thinking of the machines I could build."

Tashi rolled her eyes.

"Have you thought about the staff you want to bring with you?"

"You, of course, Chiza, if he'll come. I'll ask my mother if she wants to. Some of the crew who built the steam engine. I'll need warriors I can trust. I don't know any, but if you or Chiza can suggest people."

"I might come up with a couple of names." Tashi sighed. "About Chiza, he's the Third Prince's Right Arm. Unless he releases Chiza to you, Chiza is oathbound to serve his prince."

"I'll think of something. What would the Third Prince want that only I can give him?" Ilathia paced through the room, the dress, the weight of gold, even her disbelief that the King had done this to her, all of it vanished beneath her need.

"All right, now you're scaring me." Tashi took Ilathia's hands. "Ask, politely, don't beg, and whatever you do, don't argue with his answer. And still you don't know what Chiza wants. He's served as the Third Prince's Right Arm for years. They went to Anglia together." She squeezed Ilathia's fingers. "All I'm saying is don't get your hopes up."

Llathia nodded and blinked back tears. Tashi was right, she had no right to make decisions for Chiza without talking to him. She went out to the front room.

"Chiza?"

"Yes, my Lady." Chiza saluted her.

"It's me, llathia, the damned fool." She tilted her head back to look into his face. Chiza's mouth twitched and his eyes danced. "That's better." She took his hand and played with his fingers.

"I watched you in the arena." Chiza's rumbling voice vibrated in her chest. "You have an absolute focus on the moment very few warriors find. You bring it to building engines, to everything you do. When you learn to bring it bear on politics no one will be able to touch you."

"The First Wife will be teaching me; I hope I don't frustrate her too much."

"The King is not sending his First Wife to teach you."

Llathia looked up at him and furrowed her brow.

"He said she would be my political adviser, so I'd be a proper noble."

"He did, but Kings always mean more than what they say. The First Wife is going with you to watch you, and make sure you don't become a threat to his rule."

"You're joking." She shook his hand. "Don't tease me."

Chiza's face stayed serious. "As long as you aim for the best for the people, you'll be fine."

"You're serious." Llathia breathed in as pieces fell together in the back of her mind. She shook her head dismissing her imagining. "This is me, the young woman who builds machines and wears grease more often than jewellery."

"The First Wife was young once."

"Fine then." Llathia stamped her foot. "I will swear to you, here and now. Never will I work against what is best for Congu, and my King."

"I witness your oath." Chiza spoke reluctantly, then he sighed. "I expect you will use all your new-found power to build better machines. But if you ever need a reminder of your oath, I will be there to hold you to your word."

Llathia wrapped her arms around Chiza and put her head on his chest so she could listen to his heartbeat, strong and even. His arms came around her and for a time, the only thing in her world was his heart and hers, beating in their complicated rhythms.

"If you were free to choose." Llathia spoke the words gently, carefully. "Would you choose to come with me?"

"It isn't my choice." Chiza tightened his grip on her. "But if it was mine, I would follow you to my death."

"Thank you." llathia scrubbed at the tears on her face. "I know your oath is to serve Roger. It's important, that oath. It's important to me that you keep it, because that is who you are. The shield for my back, my Right Arm, the one who holds my heart in his hands. I will love you whatever happens."

Chiza held her a long time. His heart banged faster beneath her ear.

"When I took on the oath of a Right Arm, I didn't think I had a heart. I was stone, strong. For the King, and then for the Third Prince that was enough. Then I met you, determined, foolish, vulnerable, and I learned I did have a heart after all. All those years I thought it would make me weak, but it made me stronger. Whoever holds my oath, you hold my heart."

"Tashi is going to get bored of watching us." Llathia sighed.

"Not likely," Tashi said from behind the curtain then giggled.

Llathia laughed with her and let go of Chiza.

"It must be almost time to go to the banquet, and I can't walk in with tears on my face. I want a bit of time to putter before the plots against me begin."

Tashi washed llathia's face then kissed her hands.

"My princess, you are going cause any number of heart failures when you walk into that room. The men will be falling over themselves to claim you, and through you, Mtuak. Don't make any agreements."

"Got it, leave a trail of broken hearts." Llathia snorted. "It will only encourage them. They'll think I'm playing coy."

Tashi grinned. "I'm looking forward to watching the devastation."

They walked down the hallway, servants moved to the side of the hall and bowed to llathia. Tashi and Chiza walked behind, whispering directions to the central hall where the King was holding his banquet.

The warriors at the door saluted her with their spears, then bowed deeply before throwing the door open.

Llathia glided through the door into the huge room where every eye, from servant to King was fixed on her. If Tashi and Chiza hadn't been close behind her, she might have bolted from the room. Instead she pasted the best smile she could manage on her lips and walked over to the King.

"My King." She bowed to him. "The Lady Mtuak pledges to serve you and the Congu people."

"I accept your service." The King took her hand in his. The First Wife sat just to the King's right. She gave llathia a tiny nod.

The First Prince, to the First Wife's right stood and saluted, then the Second Prince did the same, his eyes wide. To his right, Roger beamed at her with delight.

"Lady Mtuak, allow me to introduce you to our welcome guests." The King pulled her attention back to him. He smiled crookedly. "King vvatha ssombi, our brother to the north." The man with all the gold rings stood and saluted, touching his forehead instead of his heart. "His daughter, ppomena kkitakin ssombi." The girl stared at llathia with wide eyes, wincing a little at the first name in the list of her names.

"King's Daughter kkitakin, I am happy to meet you. Perhaps you will be gracious enough to meet with my maid to discuss Sombi fashion." The girl's dress was like nothing she'd ever seen before, but it suited the child.

The girl's face brightened, and she clapped her hands before she reined herself in.

"Lady Mtuak, it would be a pleasure." Her voice carried musically across the hall.

"By good fortune, the Lady Mtuak will sit to the King's Daughter's left," The King said.

Llathia glided around the table to take the empty seat. Chiza stood behind her, solid and comforting. Tashi placed a bowl and towel in front of llathia.

"It's for washing your fingers." Kkitakin whispered. "It's a Sombi custom."

"Thank you." Llathia dipped her fingers then dried them carefully before Tashi lifted the bowl away.

The feast was long and varied. Kkitakin advised llathia to only eat a little from each dish. The girl knew the right way to do everything from eating soup to breaking open crabs. Each time llathia turned to her for advice, the child blossomed more. She glowed with the attention.

Poor child must be lonely. Llathia glanced at King vvatha systematically eating. He didn't look the type to take time to play with his daughter.

"You look like a Sombi queen," kkitakin whispered between courses. "I watched you fight that big man. You didn't even look afraid."

"I was afraid before, but then I had to act. My fear made me ready."

"I wish I could fight like that." Kkitakin plucked at her dress.

"There are all kinds of battles, my princess. I'm sure you will find yours."

The girl crinkled her face up in thought, but then the servants placed a creamy concoction in front of them, and she started into it.

"This is the best part of the feast." Kkitakin said between bites.

Llathia tried hers and had to agree.

*****

Roger couldn't see what llathia, Lady Mtuak, was up with kkitakin. How she knew to use her middle name he couldn't understand. She wasn't the girl he'd cajoled up the hill to build a steam engine. Somehow, she'd become the focal point for the most powerful people in the county.

Mtuaka had been dealt with and Roger allowed himself to relax. His father was safe, and matched King vvatha for cunning. He sighed, as glad as he was to be home, it didn't fit right.

The meal passed without him noticing any of it. *What's wrong with me? I'll have time to go hunting, relax.* The prospect didn't entice like it once would.

I want to be part of the decisions. Roger stopped with a spoon of dessert halfway to his mouth. He had definite ideas of what needed to happen, if only the King's would listen to him. He was the Third Prince, Bhansin and Tzoca would speak before him. He put his spoon down.

He'd make it happen. After all the Sombi king owed him a debt.

King vvatha stood and waved genially.

"For centuries our people have been enemies. Do any of you remember why?"

Roger shook his head along with most of the room.

"There is no record of it anywhere. Maybe it's time to let go of the habit. It's comfortable to have an honourable enemy close by, someone to keep us sharp, but who doesn't really threaten us. We can't afford such comforts anymore. The Kershian Empire crept into Harasah without us noticing. They rule the desert nations to our west, they came very close to ruling Sombi, and they were behind an attempt to take power in Congu."

He lifted his cup and sipped at it.

"Sombi is free because of help from Congu, help that came unasked for, but the conflict is not done, we'll need more help, and we'll offer aid in return. We are a people who pay our debts. Working together we can push the Empire from our shores."

The crowd applauded uncertainly. None of them were used to thinking of Sombi as anything but enemies, but the idea of a new and powerful enemy disconcerted them. Roger watched the thoughts pass across the faces of the people who led his country. King vvatha would need more than words to convince them.

"In case you think that Sombi want to rule Congu, we wouldn't know how. You'd make very poor Sombi, as we would be terrible Congu. What we need is someone who knows both countries, who puts the needs of people, even enemies before his own." The sombi king waved his hand at the people at the head table. "King Xanachi and I, along with our counsellors have a lot of work to make our borders a place of safety instead of violence. Lady Mtuak will need to offer other challenges for young warriors who, for centuries, have tested themselves against the people on the far side of the river."

Roger sighed, the man was right. Llathia was in for a difficult time, but he had the feeling this new llathia would be equal to the task.

"I haven't had much chance to talk to my brother King, but we do agree on one thing. The person who should lead our combined defense against a powerful enemy. Roger Hrona Xanachi has lived with the enemy, he understands them. He also understands us."

King Xanachi stood up as Roger's heart pounded.

"I am in agreement; our Third Prince has proven over the last weeks of his hunt that he is the man we need in place. Each country will send advisers, and we will send heralds out to our neighbours and even those further away, inviting them to send their own people to aid in the fight." He frowned and met Roger's gaze, face expressionless. "King vvatha has one other requirement for this agreement. I can't decide, Roger will have to speak his own mind, but I know he will do so with the best interests of everyone in this room in mind."

His father sat down and King vvatha's triumphant smile made Roger's gut twist. Whatever was coming wouldn't be good.

"It is tradition in both our countries," King vvatha played with his cup. "for agreements between tribes to be sealed with a joining of our peoples. I propose we seal this agreement with the marriage of Roger, Congu's Third Prince and my Daughter ppomena."

The girl's wail made Roger's hand clench until the cup in his hand shattered. He ignored the pieces stuck in his hand.

"I hate you, I hate you." The King's Daughter stood on her chair pounding on her father with her fists.

"Wait." Roger stood.

"This is necessary to bind our people." King vvatha set his face.

He thinks it will cover his debt.

"My father said it is my decision to make, but he was wrong." Roger jumped over the table and stalked toward King vvatha. The King stepped back, but his eyes had no give in them. "The person who must agree is Princess kkitakin herself."

Kkitakin paused in her screaming to look at Roger, tears running down her face.

Roger reached out to her, only then seeing the blood dripping from his hand, but he couldn't withdraw it. Kkitakin took his hand and walked across the table to Roger, pausing only to stick her tongue out at her father.

"My Queen," Roger spoke to the girl as if only the two of them were in the room. "It is a terrible decision to make. I have a friend who chose dishonour and exile to keep his sister from needing to make this decision. I can do no less. My life is in your hands. I swear by the blood shed here I will accept your will."

"I don't know what to do." Kkitakin wailed. "I don't know anything about being married. I'm scared, I don't want to. I don't." She looked down but her grip on Roger's hand tightened.

"Daughter you will—"

"I have a suggestion." Llathia spoke up. Her eyes glittered with anger. "I believe it will satisfy your desire to have a family made from our two peoples. It will also recognize that no child, not even the King's Daughter, should be married against her will."

"What is this suggestion?" King vvatha ground out the words. He obviously felt himself to be humiliated by his daughter. *Serves him right.*

"It meets both goals of your proposal." Llathia wielded her words like her spear on the sands of the arena. "That of joining our people, and of ridding yourself of a daughter you think of as an embarrassment."

King vvatha drew breath and Roger thought for the barest instant the man was going to demand satisfaction for the insult, but llathia met his glare unflinchingly.

"Very well." King vvatha huffed, then drank down his cup and threw it onto the floor. "If you can provide for both my honour and that of my daughter. I will agree."

"It is simple." Llathia's voice softened and she put her hand on kkitakin's back. The girl turned to look at llathia, never letting go of Roger's hand. She hiccoughed and took a breath.

"I am ready to listen to you."

"Very well. I propose instead of giving his daughter away in marriage, King vvatha give his daughter to become Roger Hrona Xanachi's daughter. She will be First Daughter and heir to whatever estate he has."

"I would get to live with you?" kkitakin turned her gaze on Roger. "Would you really want to be my father? You know what I'm like."

"If that is your desire, my Queen, then yes, I will gladly be father to this most courageous and honorable princess."

"And you will never, ever change your mind?"

Roger put a finger from his left hand into the blood dripping from his hand, still clutched in hers. He marked his forehead.

"I swear to you on my blood and my life, that if you become my daughter, I will be your father until I die. In sign of this I will add your name ssombi to mine and offer my name Xanachi to you."

Kkitakin pulled a shard of the cup from his hand, then slashed it across her own releasing a scream of pain and anger as she did. She put her finger in the oozing red, and marked her forehead.

"Then I accept. I will be your daughter until I die. I swear on my blood and my life. I will give you my name and take yours." She threw herself at Roger and hugged him so tightly the bones in his neck creaked. He wrapped her arms around her and held her close.

"I accept the adoption of ppomena kkitakin ssombi Xanachi binding our people in peace and in the purpose of defense against those who would take our land from us."

King vvacha sat down and glowered for a moment, then he shrugged and turned to llathia.

"I think the Mtuak are in very good hands."

"Tashi." Llathia crooked her finger. "Please arrange to bandage the wounds of the Third Prince and his First Daughter."

Chapter 13 The Next Hunt

Roger sat on a chair watching his new daughter sleep. She looked even younger and more vulnerable than ever.

"You're a brave man." His father walked in and put a hand on Roger's shoulder. "Many would have bent to the flow."

"Now what?" Roger brushed his finger across kkitakin's hair. It clung close to her scalp, just like llathia's. It felt soft to the touch. "I don't know anything about being a father."

"Neither did I." The hand squeezed. "You've already made a good start. There will be bumps along

the way, don't give up on her, or yourself. Find a way
to keep your balcony door open."

"She's used to always coming second to the rest
of the world. All I did was give her attention she
deserved."

"You kept calling her your Queen. What was that
about?"

"When the Kershians dragged me up to throw
me in front of their general, they treated me like dirt,
to them I pretty much was. I'd been left tied up in
darkness." Roger hung his head. "I had ranted and
cried, making myself a complete mess. I needed it
though, it crystalized for me what I was doing and why.
Anyway, they dropped me on the floor, still tied, still
with tear tracks on my face and my robe soaked. I'd
come to terms with being dead." Roger caressed
kkitakin's hair and her hand caught his and held it.

"Then this little whirlwind crashed onto the
scene. She shamed her father for not treating me
properly, ordered some noble to fetch clothes just like
he was a servant. Got a servant to bring water. As if
that wasn't enough, she called out the Kershians for
being cowards for leaving me tied. They didn't like that,
but they had to save face in front of the warriors. My
arms and legs wouldn't work they were so cramped
and stiff."

He shook his head and smiled, as he recalled the
moment. "So this girl, the daughter of a King, met
every one in that room head on and made them

shamed of their actions. She washed my face. I doubt she'd ever washed anyone's face before. It didn't matter, only her determination to give me dignity, to do what she thought was right. I forced my body to obey me, then I knelt in front of her and told that as long as I lived, she would be my Queen."

Roger squeezed his daughter's hand. "The Kershians thought it a great joke as they planned to kill me there and then, but King vvacha had something up his sleeve and within a few minutes all the Kershians were dead and he was retaking control of his government."

"She sounds like an amazing child."

"She is." Roger hung his head. "I'm going to have to leave her behind. I have to go to Anglia and get information on the Empire, but also where Anglia stands. Then we must assemble the defense council and find neutral territory to do it. I have an idea about that, actually. But the travel to Anglia will be too dangerous for her. I can't drag her about with no stability. But how do I tell her, after all that I said?"

"Father?" kkitakin sat up and stroked his hand. "I'm your First Daughter. I will prepare your house for you when you return, then I can help you with the council. I'll be good, I promise. How long will you be gone?"

"A month, two, three. I'm not sure."

"I'll be waiting for you."

"I know, my Queen. I'm thinking of building my Kraal in that village by the river."

"The one the Sombi's built on our side." Roger's father sounded more like his King now.

"We make it a neutral territory, the Sombi who want can stay, the Congu who want to settle can join them. We free the Congu they have working the fields, and maybe put those Mtuak warriors to work instead. It keeps them under my eye."

"Lady Ilathia will be in Mtuak governing her people, are you going to be able to work with her?"

"She not the unsure girl who came up the hill to build an engine, she's strong, but will use that to make her people stronger."

"I like her." Kkitakin lay down and snuggled against his hand. "She can help me prepare your home for when you return."

"Would you mind living with her until you get it finished?"

"That would be fun. She wants to learn about Sombi fashion. She's like a queen, I hope I grow up to be like her."

"I'm sure you will, you've already made a good start." Roger leaned down and kissed her cheek.

"Promise you won't leave without a proper goodbye."

"I promise."

When her breathing evened out, Roger recovered his hand.

212

"I have no idea what she means by a proper goodbye, I guess we'll have to talk about it tomorrow."

"You don't have to rush, vvacha and I need to work out some details."

"The Kershians will learn soon enough about the events in Sombi. They won't take being thrown out of the country lightly, so the sooner I know their likely response the better. I'll travel to Biafa and take the first ship I can find to Anglia. Just Chiza and me, so we can move fast.

"You know best."

"I'm not sure I do, but with people like kkitakin depending on me, I have to do what I can."

***

Llathia waited until she'd entered her room before she exploded.

"How dare he do that? And obviously without even consulting her." She beat a pillow with her fists.

"King vvatha may not be an enemy, but he is not your friend." Tashi sighed. "Did you have to embarrass him like that?"

"He deserved it." Llathia clenched her fist. "But more than that, he needed to be shown that Sombi and Congu are equal in this. We are not a people who will easily set aside what is right even if it will cost us dearly."

"Just days ago, you had no idea about people and their schemes, now you're skewering people and laying them out like the slimy bugs they are. What happened?"

"Chiza told me to focus on the politics around me like I did on my engine." Llathia sat on her bed and hugged the pillow. "I started thinking about people, and how what they did fit together like pieces of the engine. When everything is balanced, you get tremendous power to achieve things. If they fight each other, then at best you lose power, at worse the engine will fail completely."

She buried her face in the pillow.

"My father died because somehow he let his engine get out of balance. You know the result of that. I won't let it happen to Congu and Sombi just because I'm too scared to think."

"My princess." Tashi knelt and wrapped her arms around llathia. "While you're saving the world, take a little time to protect yourself. If too many people fear you, they won't listen."

"You're right. That's why you're so important, because you remind me of why I'm doing any of this." Llathia hugged Tashi. "I had a thought while Roger and kkitakin were talking. Do you think your sister would be willing to move to Mtuak? Your child is safe from Ntoox, and I can't bear to think of you being so far apart."

"llathia, my friend." Tashi sobbed into her shoulder. "Thank you, thank you, thank you."

Llathia held Tashi until she fell asleep. Looking at the sleeping maid, llathia reminded herself Tashi wasn't much older than she was. Though now she'd turned her focus to the people around her, she felt ancient. She didn't want to become like First Wife, brittle and discontented. Tashi and others she'd find, they would keep her human.

***

A maid knocked on the door of llathia's suite.

"Pardon, Lady Mtuak, but the little princess is inviting you to join her for breakfast. She said to bring your maid."

"Please let her know I will be coming as soon as I'm ready."

"You made an impression." Tashi leaned against the wall grinning. "What does the Lady Mtuak wear to breakfast with a princess?"

"I have no idea, but I'm sure you will make me look brilliant."

Tashi led her into the Third Prince's suite. Llathia's dress was as simple as the one the night before was elegant.

"You don't need to impress her, and if you're going to talk fashion, you want to look like you don't already have a style to cling to." Tashi had explained her choice, and llathia was for anything that allowed her to be comfortable.

"Welcome." Roger stood and bowed to her.

Llathia hadn't thought about Roger being there. Chiza stood in the corner, if he was uncomfortable with her and Roger both in the room, he didn't show it. His presence gave her courage.

"Thank you, my prince."

Kkitakin walked into the room, then ran over to llathia.

"You came."

"How could I not, when my friend invited me." Llathia sat where kkitakin told her, Tashi hesitated when the princess told her to sit too, but llathia nodded. Once Roger was in his place, kkitakin walked to the door.

"We're ready. Thank you."

Servants came in with trays of fruit and bread. A plate of meat made llathia's stomach rumble, and kkitakin giggled. When everything was set, a servant brought in a tray with bowls and towels. They washed their hands.

"Please, eat." Kkitakin told her guests. She turned to the servants. "If you would bring tea in a little bit, I would be grateful." The servants bowed and left.

"I'm impressed at how gracious you are with the servants." Tashi nibbled on a slice of fruit.

"The servants at home, what used to be home, they were the only ones who noticed me. They played with me sometimes, and never complained when I made a mess. I will always take care to treat my servants like people."

"You are wise beyond your years." Tashi saluted her.

Kkitakin ducked her head, but Ilathia could see the grin on her face. The girl chattered about Sombi clothes and what she like and didn't like about them. Roger ate, watching her as if he couldn't quite believe she was real.

"Lady Mtuak." Kkitakin stood and bowed. "I need to thank you properly for your help last night, and I want to ask a favour." She looked over at her father, and Roger nodded. "My father needs to go on a trip far away. I'm to stay in Congu and prepare a home for when he returns. Would you help me, and allow me to stay with you until it's ready?"

"Where would you like to prepare this home?" Ilathia asked the question to give herself time to adjust to the idea. How could she care for this girl? She thought about the night before. How could she not?

"There is a village on the river. The Sombi built it, but it isn't supposed to be there. My father wants to make it a place where Sombi and Congu can practice getting along. I want to make him a home there. One that is a little like Sombi, for me, and a little like Congu, for him."

"That is not far from Mtuak where I will be living. I think it would be a good place for you while you work."

"Does that mean yes?" kkitakin bounced on her toes.

"It means yes." Llathia saw Roger relax a little.

"Perhaps we should go ask the servants if the tea is ready." Tashi stood and offered a hand to kkitakin; they walked together out of the room.

"It won't be easy." Roger said. "She'll get angry and frustrated."

"I'll manage. I'll have help." Llathia glanced at Chiza and sighed.

"My prince, I have a request as well."

"Chiza." Roger said and frowned.

"Chiza." Llathia fought back the tears that threatened.

"I need him on this trip, llathia. He'll keep me safe to return to my daughter." Roger paused as if to taste the word. "But if I give a ten-year-old girl the power to choose her life, then I must give that same power to my friend."

Chiza came to the table and knelt in front of llathia. "You made me promise something."

"I did." Llathia tried to smile but her face refused. "Keep him safe, bring him home to his daughter."

"I will." Chiza lifted her chin with a finger and kissed her gently.

"It's time for *tea.*" kkitakin had her hands on her hips while Tashi carried the tray.

Chiza stood and moved to behind Roger.

"It's all right." Kkitakin dabbed a napkin on llathia's face. "Goodbyes are hard, but my father has promised a proper goodbye."

"We'll keep each other brave, shall we?" llathia reached for the girl and they embraced until kkitakin wriggled.

"The tea is going to get cold."

Chapter 14 The Proper Goodbye.

Roger looked around the large room where two days before his life had changed at a banquet. The Kings were both looking smug. The village would work as Roger proposed. The Mtuak warriors were on their way to take up the field-work. A message had already been sent ordering the Congu's release.

His brothers and a motley collection of people, from servants to the First Wife, gathered around looking expectantly at him. Kkitakin stood on the dais beside the King's chair, her lips trembling.

"First Daughter, kkitakin, my Queen." Roger fought the water in his own eyes. How had he grown so attached in just a few days? "I must go on a hunt. To find safety for our people, so we can go strong. Will you wait for me in the home you prepare?"

"I…I…" kkitakin's face crumpled. "I don't want you to go. I don't."

Roger knelt and held his daughter his own tears breaking free. She'd seen his tears; he didn't need to hide them. He held her until she stopped shaking.

"I don't want to go, but I must. You don't want to stay, but you must. Sometimes we don't like the hunt we are given."

"I understand. I'm sorry."

"kkitakin," Roger gave her an extra squeeze. "Never be sorry for being honest."

"I'm ready."

Roger stepped back.

"Father, good hunting. I will be waiting at home for you." She pulled something out of her sleeve. "If you carry this, you will have a part of me with you." Kkitakin put a find lacy kerchief in his hand.

Roger took a ring from his finger and put it on a string Chiza handed him. He looped it over kkitakin's head. "Wear this and you will have a part of me with you." Roger put his hand out to llathia.

"While I'm gone will you care for my daughter?"

"It will be my delight." Llathia's face looked ready to crumple.

"Chiza."

He surged forward and wrapped his arms around llathia and held as she sobbed. The people in the room murmured.

Roger felt an arm go around his waist. He looked down to see his daughter smiling at him.

"It's all right." She rested her head against his ribs. "I can do this now." kkitakin walked over to llathia who stood clinging to Chiza. She wrapped her arms around the woman. Llathia let go of Chiza and held on to kkitakin.

He came to stand with Roger.

"kkitakin was right. We needed this." Roger sighed. "Now we know no matter what direction we go, we'll be travelling toward home.

Other books by Alex

Series:

Calliope Books
Calliope and the Sea Serpent
Calliope and the Royal Engineers

Spruce Bay Books
Wendigo Whispers
Cry of the White Moose
Disputed Rock

The Belandria Tarot
The Devil Reversed
The Regent's Reign
The Empire Unbalanced

Stand alone books:

Generation Gap
The Gods Above
Tales of Light and Dark
Like Mushrooms (poetry and photography)
The Heronmaster
Blood and Sparkles, and other stories
Princess of Boring
By the Book
Sarcasm is My Superpower
Playing on Yggdrasil
The Unenchanted Princess

Read short stories and excerpts from his novels
at alexmcgilvery.com

A Sample from the upcoming third book in the Calliope Series.

Calliope and the Kershian Empire

Alex McGilvery

Chapter 1 Maiden Flight

The sun shining through her flat's window said the weather had cooperated for the first public flight of Her Majesty's Air Ship Adamant. Cal heaved a sigh of relief. She hadn't relished the thought of explaining to the Queen a need to postpone if the conditions weren't perfect.

Too soon to relax. The flight had to go over without a hitch. The Royal Engineers had worked incredibly hard through the winter and early spring. Their numbers had increased over with several hundred employed at factories surrounding the airfield. That didn't include the swarms of men constructing the berth for airships, each with a roof which opened.

Every time Cal thought about the creation of an air navy, the process became more complicated. She had a board in her office for the sole purpose of posting new things needing to be invented or improved. Commander Landers had taken over the day to day running of the engineers.

Today would not only be a public test of the Adamant, but of the roof system for the hanger, and the lift system. The lift had been built to get the Queen into the airship with dignity. While Cal suspected Her

Majesty could easily negotiate a rope ladder, the idea had given her nightmares.

After a quick breakfast, Cal drove her steam carriage to the air field and met with her crew in the Adamant's hanger.

Airship Captain Vittor waited with her hands behind her back- the first recruit commissioned specifically for the air navy. First Mate Jones stood behind her with the flight crew on either side of him - two engineers, the bosun, and a cook and general handyman. One engineer and the cook were also women. Cal had informed the Admiralty she planned on recruiting women as well as men. The Lord Admiral opened his mouth, then shut it and moved on to the next item.

"All right, crew." Cal smiled at them and saluted. "This is the flight you've been training for the last few months. You are the people who have come the furthest and shown the most comfort in your roles." She pointed to the Adamant. "Now get up there and do the final checks. Captain Vittor is in command, if any one of you looks to me to confirm an order, I will bounce you off the ship. If I'm feeling generous, I may wait until we land."

"Aye, Admiral." The crew said and ran to do their work. For all that half of them were older than Cal, she still thought of them as kids. Maybe it went with the rank.

The Queen's guard arrived after all the lists had been run through twice. The ground crew polished the lift until it shone, then laid a carpet on the walkway to make the footing better.

"Everything ready?" The Sergeant of the Queen's Guard stood beside her and craned his neck to look at the airship.

"It is."

"Six crew and six passengers. That's not as much at the Ferandican airship carries."

"I decided to travel light. It gives us more options."

"Options?" The Sergeant frowned. "Her Majesty needs to be kept safe."

"She will be." Cal waved around the building. "Everything in here has been inspected and re-inspected. The crew is the best of the lot, and not one person in here would hesitate to put their life on the line for the Queen."

"Very good." The Sergeant nodded at Cal and relaxed slightly. "The Queen is on her way."

"Thank you." Cal turned to a man carrying a board with pen and paper. "Whistle the crew into formation, Petty Officer."

The ground crew formed up with the flight crew in front. They waited for her Majesty to arrive.

"Her Majesty, Admiral Royal." The Sergeant announced her and everyone in the hanger stood to attention.

"Impressive." The Queen walked along the lines of the crew. "You look sharp and ready. Your Admiral's trust in you is well placed."

"Your Majesty." Captain Vittor bowed. "Would you prefer to fly first, or tour the hanger?"

"We would think as Airship Captain; you'd want to show off your ship."

"I do, your Majesty, but respectfully, the ground crew are no less members of the Air Navy. Without them, we couldn't fly. I wouldn't be a good Captain if I short-changed them."

"Very well, Captain Vittor. We shall tour the hanger, then fly in your ship." The Queen walked through the hanger asking questions about the equipment for a full hour before the tour led her to the lift.

"The lift will carry four people at a time, your Majesty." The Chief Petty Officer opened the gate. "Your guards have informed me you will board last. If you will stand behind the white line on the floor we will know you are safely clear of the machinery while we work." He bowed to her as she moved to her place.

The lift didn't move very quickly, but with only three trips, all the people for today's flight boarded the Adamant in less than fifteen minutes.

"Amazing. I expected the floor to move under my feet." The Queen looked around.

"With the size of the Adamant small changes in weight don't have much effect. Like boarding a ship of the line compare to a dinghy." Cal led her Majesty to a chair set by a floor to ceiling window. The panes of glass curved around the front of the gondola. She nodded at Captain Vittor. "Captain, you have command."

"Aye, Admiral." She leaned to speak into a tube. "Ground crew, open the roof. Stand by to release anchor ropes."

The Queen's eyes widened as the roof moved out of the way. It went quicker than Cal's barn roof with cables winching it down as the pressure in the cylinders dropped.

"Release anchor ropes."

The ship bobbed up slightly as the ropes' tension vanished. The crew pulled the ropes up and coiled them out of the way before closing the hatches.

"Engine room one, turn prop. Engine room two, turn prop." The sound of the engines came through the wall, but muffled, more a hum than a howl.

"Engines to quarter power." The Captain pulled on the levers and the flukes at the stern angled to send the Adamant up. She worked the rudder with her feet to turn to fly over the city, and more specifically, the royal palace.

Two hours later the Adamant hovered over the hanger as the crew dropped the ropes. She was winched down into her berth and the roof closed.

"That was extraordinary." The Queen turned to Captain Vittor. "My compliments to you and your crew for a smooth flight."

"Your Majesty." Captain Vittor bowed and picked up a small box from beside her chair. "In honour of your first flight, the crew of the Adamant, flight and ground both, would like to present you with these wings." She opened the box to show the Queen before handing it over.

Cal had negotiated for hours with the Queen's Guard to allow the presentation to be made directly to the Queen. From the delight on her Majesty's face, it had been worth the aggravation.

"That went well." Cal stood watching the crew put the ship to rest. Captain Vittor leaned against the wall beside her.

"Not bad for a short cruise, but we didn't need to light the fires on the boilers, and we didn't push any limits. Not that we could with her Majesty aboard. I'd like to have permission to put the Adamant through her paces. Too late to make many changes to her sister ships, but the next group to be built need to be an improvement."

"Permission granted." Cal glanced over at the Captain. "Hard to believe six months ago you were running a shop with your husband."

"Still am, or at least he is. The shop is his thing more than mine. I liked the organizing, making sure everything worked together. I answered the ad on a bet. We'd had an argument over how much cheese to stock. He told me if I passed the entry, he'd do everything I told him."

"Does he?"

"What would be the fun in that?" Captain Vittor laughed. "He's my husband, not my crew. Besides he's right at least as often as I am. The children help him out. My oldest son is already counting the years before he can enlist, but that only makes him more determined to work hard to prove he can."

"Captain, the Adamant's sister ships will be finished within the month. Their crews are already training hard. As soon as they are launched, we'll set the keels for the next group. Have any recommendations you want to make ready as soon as possible."

"Aye Admiral."

***

Cal washed up then sat at her desk and ate while she worked. She had an idea about using a version of the Kite to fly from airships. The problem was how to get the person and the Kite back on the ship. Reconnaissance wouldn't be very helpful if they couldn't get the report without landing to pick up the crew member.

She'd thought about dangling ropes, but with the person being under the Kite, that wasn't practical. Landing on top of the airship might work, though it would mean getting the airship below the Kite. That might be as bad as landing. The Kite depended completely on air currents. Cal had tried a few more flights, taking off from the roof of the Academy, but without an updraft, they were short.

Maybe more of a boarding tactic?

Cal pushed the drawings aside and reluctantly pulled out the journal where she'd been tracking the progress of the Air Navy. Each ship needed eight to ten crew members for anything more than a sightseeing cruise. Right now, they had six for the Adamant, and six each for the Peridot and the Opal. The ground crew was another eight to ten per ship at minimum.

The hangers they'd built would hold the three ships on the way, but larger ships wouldn't work. Even now, they had issues with the roof and walls which had slowed construction. How were they going to build and maintain airships without the shelter of a hanger? Those hangers required their own crew to maintain, apart from the ground crew.

The plans for the Wellington sat on the desk, but Cal hadn't worked up the nerve to take her over for the support role. She'd have to talk to the Admiralty about it, and soon if Captain Vittor was going to take longer cruises.

Cal noted in the journal the things she needed to do and the timeframe. Get tweaks for the next three ships. Assign a vice-Admiral, Captain Vittor would be good for that position in a year or two. The item on the list Cal hated was the one about how to arm the ships. The Crown Prince's original vision had been scientific expeditions, showing off the strength of Anglia to the nations around her.

Only from what Bri told her before he returned to Kershia, war was coming. The Kershian Empire wouldn't hesitate to build floating warships. If Anglia didn't have a response, the result would be devastating. She'd drawn a few sketches, but that wasn't what she wanted. Soon it wouldn't matter.

Less heartbreaking was the defense needs of the airship. It was only as strong as its envelope, a break or a tear and it would be grounded at best. Cal played around with multiple envelopes and layers between them to lessen the impact of an attack. If the ship carried a way to patch an envelope, it would help. Maybe there was a way to put the hydrogen under pressure and carry extra?

***

"Her Majesty was delighted with the tour." The Lord Admiral beamed at Cal. "The funding for the Air Navy will continue as it is for the moment. All new shipbuilding will be airships for the next couple of years. We need a reserve of ships for training and to replace old and damaged vessels."

"We will have three operational before summer. The keels will be laid for the next trio as soon as the first lot are launched. Training continues, so we will have crews for each airship. Captain Vittor is going to put Adamant through her paces and learn what can and can't be done. For support, I'd like to use the Wellington as a mobile base for the airships. She has a large foredeck which will hold the gondola, and sufficient cargo room for parts for repair and maintenance."

"How is the captain of the Wellington going to feel about this?"

"He was interested in the idea. After taking on the Impossible, he was already thinking about slight modifications to make such operations easier in the future."

"Can we let her go without damaging our domestic response, Jack?" The Lord Admiral looked over at their colleague who ran the domestic Navy.

"Certainly. It makes sense to expand the capability of the airships if we are going to use them. Probably want more than one ship in the support role soon, but the Wellington's a good start. Captain has a solid head on his shoulders."

"Very well." The Lord Admiral made a note. "Please send him his new orders. Cal, let the shipyard know what you need from them. Go supervise if you need."

"Aye, Sir."

"Right then, we need to look at the recruitment numbers. If there are people in the Navy who can command airships, we need to find them and get them training." Vice-Admiral Peysk put his elbows on the table. "We will also need to find people to replace them. Given the success Cal's show with her recruiting, I think we need to broader our horizons. We have no ban on women in the Navy, and there are a few who go through the Academy each year, but we don't actively recruit them. That needs to change."

"Look at what the Air Navy has been doing, and use what you can." The Lord Admiral pinched the bridge of his nose. "You all know where we're headed. We need to be ready to defend ourselves and our allies. This next war will be decided in the air as much as on the land or sea."

The discussion roved through the different branches, all who struggled to bring new ideas to bear on old problems.

"Cal, if you could wait a moment after we dismiss?" The Lord Admiral looked around the table. "Very well, dismissed." The others filed out of the room.

"Yes, Sir?"

"You've been working straight through since last summer. I'm concerned you haven't even taken a weekend off to look at your country estate. Dedication is all well and good, but if you work yourself into an early grave, where will we be?" He leaned against the table. "Take a week while your people do what they need to do. Then you'll be fresh when their reports hit the table. It will take that long to get orders to the Wellington anyway."

"Yes, Sir." Cal thought of going home to an empty flat and eating at her work table. "I think you're right, a change of scenery will be welcome. I've been doing nothing but work. My studio and the flat have nothing but plans for airships. I need to do some other drawing before I forget how to do it." Cal ran her fingers through her hair. "Prince Alfred is throwing a ball to raise interest in his art gallery project. I will leave following that event and return in a week. Flying The Impossible down there will be fun and let me try out some new gadgets."

"Enjoy yourself. If things go the way we fear, you may not have much more opportunity to do so."

***

"The Lady Admiral Marquis Calliope Shillingsworth"

Cal glided through the door as she was announced. The months of attendance at these events made walking in her gowns as natural as her stride through the workshops she oversaw.

The men and women in the room looked at her out of the corner of their eyes or boldly stared. Neither bothered her anymore. She'd been labelled a coward, a traitor, and now a heroine. None of the labels fit, she had better things to do than try to explain herself to those more interested in scandal than truth. Cal smiled, stopped and chatted with people, listened in to conversations around her.

The threat of war led the list of topics with the least informed being the most vehement in their opinions.

"The Empire has a fleet of twenty floating warships. We need to put every penny into building our own forces. The merchants will have to accept a higher tax."

"Taxing the merchants into the ground will only mean we won't be able to get the materials we need."

"The Empire is all bluff and bluster. They'd never dare challenge Anglia."

"We should send an airship over the Imperial Palace and drop a bomb on it."

Cal gave up and rolled her eyes. Prince Alfred saw and winked at her. She sighed and started her counter-attack.

"Who burns their house down to get rid of a mouse?" Cal twirled her wine glass in her fingers.

"What are you talking about?" The man looked like a tomato in a suit. A baron from the west of Anglia, if Cal remembered.

"The Empire is still a mouse. A nuisance, a time will come when they may become a lion, but until then we must not damage our own home. Why do their work for them?"

The man frowned and Cal swore she heard gears grinding behind his wrinkled brown face.

"The best response is to show we aren't afraid of them. If we panic and scurry about, we'll only encourage them."

"I suppose." The man wandered away, but Cal heard him quoting her word for word a few minutes later.

She held the same wine glass later in the evening when Prince Alfred made his impassioned speech about the importance of art. The people in the room applauded politely, but most were more concerned with their bluster or predictions of doom.

Cal stood forward to the podium when the Prince waved her forward.

"Good work, your Highness, you've softened them up for me."

"Are you sure? They don't seem impressed."

"Now it's my turn." She bowed to him. "You did better than you think."

Cal face the crowd, most who still chatted with the people beside them. She took a sip of the wine, then set it down.

"I've been walking through the room and listening." Cal sent her voice bouncing off the walls. "I hear a lot of concern about impending war. As the Admiral of Her Majesty's Air Navy the prospect is not one which makes me happy. Sure, we have airships, canons, warships, the best men and women warriors on the planet, but even for the victors, war is destructive.

"This is why I am here to speak to you of Anglia's secret weapon against those who would destroy us." Cal smiled tightly as every eye in the room focused on her. Secrets were powerful. "I could talk to you about the airship that many of you saw flying above the city not long ago, or that the Queen herself flew on that airship. Maybe I should mention the others almost ready to launch. Perhaps brag about the hundreds of engineers who work daily to improve our readiness to protect ourselves." Cal waved her hand dismissively.

"That is all true, and even important, but not the thing which will confound the Empire's ambition and that of any nation which sets itself against us. That thing is the courage of our people. Not just our fighting forces, but the baker who gets up before dawn to light the ovens, the mechanic who keeps the trains running. The artist who paints visions of glory and hope. Each one of you already supports the baker and mechanic and all the others who daily make this country a wonderful place to live.

"Artists, however, are unique. We won't perish from the lack of art, but as an artist myself I will say we will be diminished. Now, in the face of uncertainty, is the time to invest in those who show us the beauty and courage of our land. Showing off our art, encouraging those who create it tells those who would be our enemies that we are not afraid. We will drink our tea, eat scones and jam, and admire the work of our artists.

What better way can we respond to show our defiance?"

"In the fall, I pledged to Prince Alfred the sum of 20,000 sovereigns to start the work of building a place to showcase the work of Anglia's artists, past and present. I've been thinking about that amount and have come to the conclusion I made a terrible mistake. To correct it, I am announcing I will be giving to the Royal Gallery the sum of 50,000 sovereigns. The Crown is funding airships, training, naval vessels, and the rest. It is up to us to fund our secret weapon and show the world we are not frightened by bullies, even if they call themselves an Empire."

Cal stepped away from the podium, curtsied deeply to Prince Alfred who stared at her in shock.

By the end of the evening, several hundred thousand in pledges had been made.

"I have some land, and an architect who's done some preliminary plans." Prince Alfred said as he bowed over Cal's hand. "With the pledges from this evening we will be able to break ground before the summer."

"I am glad to hear that, your highness."

"I hear you are off to your estate for a well-deserved rest."

"I've left instructions with my business manager. He will pay out whatever amount you need to keep the project moving."

Cal took the coach back to her flat, and after she was freed from her gown, dismissed the maid for the night and went to sleep.